Sophia James

Unlaced, Undressed... Undone!

MASQUERADING MISTRESS

ISBN-13: 978-0-373-29475-6
ISBN-10: 0-373-29475-1
9 780373 29475 6
50599
EAN
HHIFCART875

"She said she had once been... intimate with you."

"You are telling me this woman said that I was her lover?" Thornton shouted.

"She did."

"Is she simple?"

"She definitely does not give that impression."

"Ugly, then?" Thornton hated to even utter the question, given the state of his own face, but he had to know what he was up against.

"Caroline is one of the most beautiful women to have ever graced London."

He had never been a vain man, but he had not left his home for close on twelve months now, ignoring the whispered rumors that swirled around his name.

Reclusive. Damaged. Solitary.

And now to be thrust back into society because some featherbrained woman had decided to lie about her sexual favors and others had decided to listen? For just a moment he was...curious, an emotion that he had not felt in years.

* * *

Masquerading Mistress

Harlequin® Historical #875—December 2007

Praise for Sophia James

Ashblane's Lady

"An excellent tale of love, this book is more than a romance; it pulls at the heartstrings and makes you wish the story wouldn't end."

—*Romantic Times BOOKreviews*

Sophia James

MASQUERADING MISTRESS

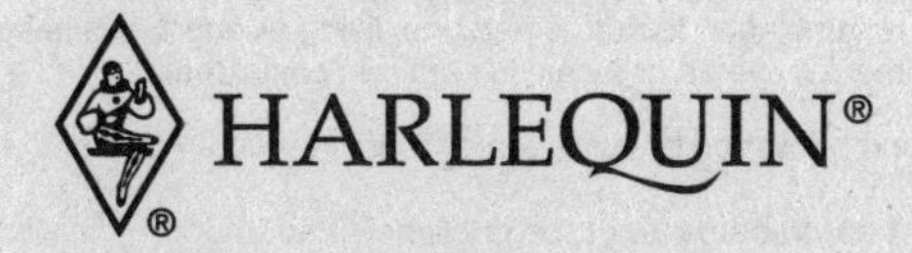

TORONTO • NEW YORK • LONDON
AMSTERDAM • PARIS • SYDNEY • HAMBURG
STOCKHOLM • ATHENS • TOKYO • MILAN • MADRID
PRAGUE • WARSAW • BUDAPEST • AUCKLAND

ISBN-13: 978-0-373-29475-6
ISBN-10: 0-373-29475-1

MASQUERADING MISTRESS

This edition published by arrangement with Harlequin Books S.A.

www.eHarlequin.com

Printed in U.S.A.

Available from Harlequin® Historical and
SOPHIA JAMES

Fallen Angel #171
Ashblane's Lady #838
Masquerading Mistress #875

To my twin sister, Karen

Prologue

1794
England

His hand brushed the side of her face and he smiled as she skipped away, the sun in her red-blonde hair. To take hold of Eloise St Clair was like containing smoke. She never stopped. Never waited for him to catch her up or slow her down.

Even here after their tryst in the woods she didn't tarry, her jacket buttoned and her boots relaced. Maxwell hoped that she felt the same joy as he did in their lovemaking and the thought worried him. Putting anxiety aside, he reached into his pocket. The trinket lay against the silk inner lining and he could feel its warmth.

A sign.

That she might say yes.

'Eloise.' He hated the catch he could hear in his voice.

'What is it, Maxim?' Her pet name for him grated against the onslaught of his early manhood.

'I brought you something. Us something,' he amended as she walked back towards him, the hint of gold in his hand catching her attention as no words ever could.

'A present?' Now he had her full regard.

'To keep me close.' Handing over the locket, he watched as she flipped open the catch.

'You drew these of us?'

He nodded. 'It could be like a ring, Elli. Like a betrothal ring, 'til we reach our majority and can be married.'

'Your parents disapprove of me. My father told me he had heard it in church and I am certain that he would not lie.'

A shadow passed over the sun, hiding the blue of the day beneath greyness, leaching out its warmth.

'When we are older nobody can tell us what to do.'

She shook her head; the red-gold curls that spilled out from a flimsy band of velvet reaching almost to the line of her waist. 'Nay, your mother will take you off to London and you will forget me. I am only the Reverend's daughter, after all.'

For the first time since they had met two years ago Maxwell heard vulnerability in her words and, because having the upper hand with Eloise was so unusual, he pressed further an argument that he might otherwise never have used.

'Let's bind ourselves to a troth right now. Here. In the

woods today.' He pulled a small knife from his pocket. 'In blood. Yours and mine.'

The spurt of fire in her eyes egged him on. Placing the blade against the skin on his wrist, he ran it clean across the blueness of vein. Blood trickled down the inside of his palm and fell in droplets from his fingers.

He was relieved when she offered him her hand and even more relieved when she did not faint as sharp steel bit in. Mingling blood, he pressed their arms into the shape of a cross. Symbolic. Eternal.

'If my parents do not allow us to marry, we could always elope?'

'You think they would not follow us, Maxwell, would not pull us apart with the influence that they wield?' She used his name, his real name, and the look in her dark eyes was sad. Fey. Knowing.

Unsettled, he pulled back, surprised at the amount of blood that had soaked into the linen of his shirt.

'I will walk you home.'

'No. It's quicker if I go by myself.' A light touch of her thumb on his cheek and she was gone, the ache in his wrist intensifying as he watched her run.

Chapter One

April 1816
Penleven Castle, Cornwall

'She said *what...*?' The Duke of Penborne's shout echoed around the antechamber and Leonard Lindsay stepped back.

'Caroline Anstretton said that she had once been... intimate with you. She did qualify that it was no longer the case, but her tone of voice was such that most people present guessed that she still harboured at least some affection.'

Hearing the words a second time made little difference to the scale of Thornton's anger and, making an effort to temper it, he tried again. This was hardly his cousin's fault, after all, and he was long past the stage of caring enough to shoot the messenger when the news was bad.

'You are telling me this woman said that I was her lover?'

'She did.'

'Is she simple?'

'She definitely does not give that impression.'

'Ugly, then?' He hated to even utter the question given the state of his own face, but he had to know what he was up against.

'She is one of the most beautiful women to have ever graced London. I have heard that said time and time again since she arrived here and I would guess that, even given the enormity of her confession, she would have a hundred takers for her favours were they given half the chance.'

'The chance?'

'The chance to get close to her. Whether anyone is enjoying her favours already is anyone's guess, for she is somewhat...experienced in her pursuit of men.' His voice lowered as he continued in the fashion of one who would hate to be thought of as a gossip, but who, in fact, relished the scandal and prattle of society. 'It is said that she was married briefly to a French general.'

'A busy woman, then.' Thornton's irony was lost on his cousin and, smiling, he brought one hand up across his cheek, the scarred ridge of raised flesh rough against his fingers. Cannon fire had a way of making certain that you never forgot its power, and even two years after the church had been blown up in his face he could still smell the singe of burning flesh, still feel the agony of his melting skin and the blackened weeks of delirium that had followed.

Five months of fighting his way back out of hell. And then a further seven months of seeing that hell reflected in the mirror every time he looked at himself while convalescing in L'Hôpital des Anges in the south-west of France.

He grimaced. He had never been a vain man, but he was not ready to return to society and to all that it entailed.

Not yet.

But when?

Closing his eyes against the thought, he moved towards the window, liking the sound of the wild sea echoing beneath the ramparts of Penleven Castle.

Home.

Safety.

A place where he could hide and lick his wounds and regroup. He had not left it for close on twelve months now, ignoring the whispered rumours that swirled around his name.

Reclusive. Damaged. Solitary.

And now to be thrust back into society because some feather-brained woman had decided to lie about her sexual favours and others had decided to listen...?

Caroline Anstretton. Her face was not difficult for him to imagine. She would have alabaster pale skin and eyes that were threaded in pity.

Lord!

He had come home for peace and quiet and solitude. And to hide.

There. He admitted it to himself as the fragile first beams of spring sunshine slanted across the skin on his left hand. Spring. A new beginning, and all he could feel was the bone-cold chill of winter and the stripped bareness of scars opaque against the slight warmth of sun.

Leonard moved uneasily behind him. Reaching out for the brandy, Thornton imagined, and topping up on courage. His cousin's complexion looked more sallow each time he had seen him of late and he wondered if he was ailing. Perhaps Penleven brought out the worst in him with the lost possibility of any inheritance. He had, after all, been the custodian of the castle for five years when military duty had kept him in Europe. Thorn wondered how he would have felt had the situation been reversed and decided that Leonard's melancholy was probably wholly understandable, for a family stipend of limited means and the necessity to be beholden to the wealthier members of the family could hardly be easy.

With measured care he stood, a cane taking the weight from his left leg.

'I am certain that this whole ridiculous accusation will blow over before the week's end and those who have deigned to take notice of such nonsense will have moved on to the next scandal.' He heard the irritation in his voice and tried to temper it as his cousin looked up.

'If it were not for Excelsior Beaufort-Hughes, indeed it might well do so.'

'Beaufort-Hughes?'

'It seems that he almost won the girl's hand in a game of whist and has been complaining loudly about the fact that a duke of the realm should be openly consorting with a young lady of such…dubiousness in the first place.'

'A young lady?'

'I would put her at no more than twenty.'

'And her family? Where are they?'

'She has a brother. And his reputation is as disreputable as hers. He's a card player.'

A gambler and a liar!

For just a moment he was…curious, an emotion that he had not felt in years, and he savoured the tiny echo of it. Anything was better than the dulling ennui he had been plagued with of late.

But why would the girl lie?

Because she did not expect him to come and refute any untruth. The answer came easily.

'You could return with me, Thornton, to sort the whole thing out. Not good for the Lindsay name, you understand, just to leave it as it is.'

Thornton forced back mirth. The Lindsay name? Lord, if Leonard knew even a half of the things he had done on the continent under the sanctity of country and crown…

He flexed the fingers on his right hand and then drew

them back into a fist as he mulled over his cousin's ludicrous notions of manners and protocol. Vague social niceties defining lives lost in far-off lands.

Lillyanna's life.

His life. By degrees.

Of a sudden he was unreasonably tired by the Anstretton girl's nonsense and by his cousin's interpretation of a stain on the name of Lindsay. And to be dragged up to London for such a flimsy reason made everything doubly worse.

And yet, running his fingers across the ache in his thigh, there was something about this whole débâcle that he found…stimulating. A beautiful woman who would lie in front of an assembly of people and expect no redress? A woman with a penchant for theatrics and a family more unusual than his own? Interest blossomed. What possible circumstances could have brought her to this pass?

He smiled.

The spy in him was not so easily dismissed, after all, and the puzzle of Caroline Anstretton beckoned with a jarring unrightness.

No more than twenty and ruined.

Beautiful. Deceitful.

And desperate. He wondered where that thought had come from even as he imagined the personal effort required for a stay in London. Lord, the memory of the last time he had ventured up to the city was still raw in his mind. The stares and the sympathy, the artfully disguised condolences of those who had known him before his accident and the hypocrisy of whispered truths as he passed them by. *'He used to be... He once was... I remember when...'*

One week, he told himself even against his better judgement.

One week in the city and then he would return home.

She should not have said it.

Should not have dragged the name of a man lauded for his very solitude into the sticky equation of survival.

But she had had no option.

The Earl of Marling, Excelsior Beaufort-Hughes, was as old as he was obnoxious, and, as she had held the lace hanky to her nose, she had said it. To everyone at the house party of Lady Belinda Forsythe.

'Thornton Lindsay, the Duke of Penborne, was my lover once and after him there is no way on earth that I could ever deign to sleep with you.'

Caroline still remembered the silence after her utterance, the shocked gasp of her audience and the hatred of her aged would-be suitor as he thrust her brother's gambling chit forward and again demanded redress.

Redress in the form of Caroline's body.

It was the lateness of the hour that had saved them as those full in their cups had drifted off to the next social engagement, leaving Thomas and her to sort out the whole sorry affair.

Sorted! Lord. That had been over a week ago and now the Duke of Penborne was due at the Wilfreds' ball at any moment. Her heart began to hammer. As the most famous recluse of his time he could hardly be overjoyed by her false proclamation. Lady Dorothy Hayes, an elderly woman of some notoriety, was standing next to her and spoke the words she was sure everyone else in the room was thinking.

'Lindsay has barely left Cornwall since returning wounded from the Continent. He was a captain in the army under Wellington, you understand.' She paused for effect before continuing. 'An intelligence officer, if the rumours are to be believed, and there are many who say he lost his heart in the role. The Heartless Duke: a man with neither the inclination nor the desire to keep company with others.'

Sweat pooled in the hollow between Caroline's breasts as the buzz of conversation became louder. She had never enjoyed the good will of the society doyennes since arriving in London; solid women with the weight of manners and propriety on their shoulders and with husbands who wielded influence in court. And yet, conversely, she had never been quite as isolated as she found herself now. A self-confessed harlot and one abided only because of the intrigue of scandal. She stood now in the shadows of a netherworld, a darker corner of society where card sharks and pimps lingered around the bright glitter of respectability, garnering the crumbs of small outcries and using them to their own advantage.

A fallen woman.

Shoved away from properness by circumstance.

She shook away introspection and thought she might be ill as the line of people parted and a tall figure with his cloak collar raised high around his face limped forward. It should take Lindsay about six seconds to name her a liar for the gathering silence all around was more telling than any whispered gossip.

She could barely see his face between the folds of material and his arm weighed heavily on an ebony cane as he came to her side. Pushing back the cloth, he ignored the collective gasp of shock, indifference in his gait as he made an easy bow in front of her. His left cheek was crossed with raised scars and he wore a leather patch on the eye above. The buttons on his jacket caught the light from the candelabra above and sent a blade of lustre across the floor, its edges stained in rainbow.

'I have it on good authority that you are Caroline Anstretton?' A sharp hint of question filled his words and when she met his glance she almost recoiled, one dark gold eye imprinted with such startling and brittle indifference. 'And I understand that you and I share a history.'

His gaze moved across her in a desultory fashion, taking in the over-made face, she guessed, before his glance fell to her hands. She stopped wringing her kerchief immediately and tried to salvage the situation.

'You may not remember me?' The sound of pleading made her voice high and wobbly so she tried again, taking no notice of the titter of the women around her. 'Of course you must be extremely busy…'

'I doubt, madam, that I would ever forget you.'

With his glance running suggestively over her body, Caroline batted her eyelashes and dredged up the last of her acting skills. 'I can see that you fun with me, Your Grace.'

Her teeth worried her upper lip now in sheer desperation and she was pleased for the length of the wig she wore, its bundling red curls hiding a growing shame.

Anything to shelter behind. This whole charade was a lot harder to perform in front of a man whose face espoused a keen intelligence and a hint of some other emotion she could not quite fathom. Her heart began to pound as the voices around her became louder and people moved back. *Please help me, God,* she thought to herself and took a deep breath of air. *Help me, help me, help me.*

Unexpectedly his one visible eye caught hers, sharp irritation overlaid by perplexity.

'Was I a good lover?'

The question was said in the tone of one who did not give a damn for the reply and in that second Caroline understood two things: he had absolutely no care for what society thought of him and he was far more dangerous than any man she had ever met.

Her bravado faltered, Excelsior Beaufort-Hughes's toothless grin suddenly less frightening than the steely stare of the man opposite her.

She felt strange, dislocated and uncertain. What manner of man would leave himself so open to insult and be amused by it?

Slowly she rallied. All of London knew her to be the fallen and discarded mistress of the Duke of Penborne. And worse. But this war-weary soldier-Duke had a home here. A place. And with the scars of battle drawn upon him, she knew without a doubt that he must have suffered.

'You were the most competent lover I have ever had the pleasure of being with.' She said the words carefully, so that even those far from them could, in the silence, hear the statement.

And for the first time she saw a glimmer of amusement.

'How old are you?'

The question was unexpected.

'Twenty.'

'Old enough to know, then, that she who plays carelessly with fire must expect to be burned by it.'

He looked around at the pressing crowd, disdain in his eye and distance, though in the tightening of his lips she sensed a quieter anger, a deliberation that gave her the singular impression of not being quite as detached as others might have thought him. Many had dropped their gaze from his and shuffled nervously.

He had once been beautiful. So beautiful that she had heard many a whispered confidence of hopeful girls.

She wished that he might lower his collar so she could see the true extent of his damage. But he stood there with his ruined face and his ebony cane and by the sheer and brutal force of his personality he dared the room not to comment on the changes upon him that war had wrought.

Such a victory she thought, and admiration surfaced.

'Perhaps we could come to an arrangement.'

'Pardon?' His suggestion puzzled her.

'You seem to be between...protectors and I find myself interested in being reacquainted with your bounteous charms. Where is your brother?' He was still, waiting, danger harnessed only by the thread of circumstance.

'I am not certain that you quite understand the situation, Your Grace...' she began, but the sentiment died in her throat as Thomas pushed through the gathering crowd from the direction of a gaming room.

'You are the brother?' Thornton Lindsay's voice was barely civil and Tosh looked as nervous as she was.

He nodded and flushed.

'Your sister has told the world that she and I were once...close,' he enunciated carefully. 'I thought perhaps we could be so again.'

'No.' The pulse in her brother's throat raced.

'No?' A languid humour replaced anger as his right hand reached out to the lace on Caroline's bodice and traced the line of her bosom.

A challenge. Pure and simple.

And when Tosh came forward it took the Duke of Penborne less than five seconds to lay him out cold on the parquet floor. No thrown punches either, just a twist of his hands against the pulse in his neck and Thomas lay still.

Silence blanketed the large salon as he bent to retrieve his cane. 'When he wakes up, send him to my apartments. I shall be happy to give him a chit for any damage he may have incurred.' He pulled a card from his pocket as he spoke. 'Here is my direction. I shall expect you both tomorrow at two in the afternoon.'

And then he was gone, a solitary figure making his way slowly down the marbled staircase.

Bested. They had been bested by a master at the game and so, so easily. She looked neither left nor right as she helped Thomas up and they departed.

'I do not think Penborne is quite the man we thought him to be, Tosh.' Caroline dipped the cloth into cold water and brought it to the bump on his head, gained when he fell at the Duke's hand.

'And what sort of a man was that?'

'A man who would do anything to avoid a public scandal. A man who would stay in his castle in Cornwall and ignore the issues of society.'

Her brother rolled up from his place on the sofa, the dimples in his cheeks easily seen. 'Well, then, if you had not baited Excelsior Beaufort-Hughes in the first place, none of this other fracas would have been necessary. My hand was full and his was the next throw. I could have beaten him easily if you had just been patient.'

'Patient? You had already lost your winnings for the last week. And the fellow next to you had a full flush.'

Thomas paled. 'He could not have. I held three aces.'

'But not the ace of hearts. It was left in the cards that you opted to pass. If I had not knocked the table as I stood and proclaimed Lindsay as my lover, I might well be ensconced this minute in the Marling country estate and there would be little that you or the law could have done to change it.'

'God help me,' Thomas whispered and his eyes met hers. Dark blue orbs mixed with grey. The perfect rogue. Her beloved twin brother.

'Well, we cannot stay here any longer, Caro. With the Duke a damn pugilist we'd better be gone from here by the morning. Though perhaps we should take him up on his offer of money.'

Nodding, Caroline kissed him on his forehead and declared his injuries healed. 'After which, we will leave for Bath. Helena Alexander has asked us down for her soirée with the promise of a few nights' accommodation attached. She is a pretty girl, Thomas, and kind with it—I have seen how she looks at you.'

Crossing to the mirror, she loosened the pins that held her wig in place and shook it free. Her own corn-blonde hair was plastered to her scalp, the heat of the day apparent. Leaning over, she ruffled her fingers through the roots and almost instantly the curls began to reassert themselves. The heavy rouge she wore looked incongruous against the short elfin cut and she smiled.

'I like England. I like everything about it. It feels like…home.'

'Pity it's no longer ours, then.' Her brother walked to the sideboard and poured a large brandy. Caroline frowned. He had been drinking too much lately and she could hear more and more a note of desperation in the tone of his voice.

Ever since the death of their mother.

Ever since they had fled Paris, penniless and hunted.

'There are other ways to deal with our problems, Tosh.'

His eyes flashed. Real anger evident. 'How, Caroline?' He seldom called her by her full name and she knew now that his patience was stretched, the dark streaks of dye in his hair making him look tired.

'We could hit Lindsay for a large amount. He is rumoured to be as rich as Croesus. With money we could change identities, leave London and begin anew somewhere else.'

'He knocked me down in a minute flat. I can hardly heavy-hand him into giving more than he wants to.'

'Let me do it, then. Let me go to see him.'

'You?'

She heard laughter in his tone and smiled. 'I can be awfully persuasive.'

'I am not sure. He seems...menacing.'

'But I cannot imagine that he would hurt a woman.'

When her brother hesitated she knew that she had him, and, looking back at the mirror, she saw a shining anticipation in her dark blue eyes.

She wanted to see Thornton Lindsay again. Wanted to understand better what made him so...beguiling. Even scarred and hurt he had a strength that was undefinable and a power that made others look ordinary. Masculinity and distance and the sculptured fineness of what was left of his face made him more attractive again.

She would wear her light blue dress with the half-boots that added a few inches to her height. And for extra measure she would carry a rock in her reticule. If he became difficult, she would need something to contain him.

His quick subduing of her brother came to mind as a warning and she pushed the thought back.

One chance. One meeting. Destiny tore apart common sense and she began to imagine things that she had long thought dormant inside of her.

And then just as quickly dismissed them.

Chapter Two

She should not have come.

She knew it the moment the Duke of Penborne shepherded her into his library and closed the heavy door behind her.

Today he was dressed entirely in black and the pantaloons he wore harked more of the country than the city in both cut and style. With his cape removed she saw that his dark hair was long, tied at the nape with a sliver of leather, neither carefully attended nor fussily arranged.

Uncertainly she clutched her reticule in front of her, the light from the window falling on to the scars of his face and adding mystery to an arrant and blatant dangerousness.

What was she doing here? she asked herself, as courage faltered. What stupidity had overcome her to make her even think that she could outsmart this man? God help me, she cursed beneath her breath and felt a rising dread, but she had brought the charade thus far and had to finish the thing off. Even a small amount of money would bolster a flagging purse. Carefully she removed her coat, the thick wool a shield to her daintier charms.

Tossing her head, she reverted to character and brought her hand to her throat, thrusting out her bosom, and pleased when his eye wandered to that part of her anatomy.

'My brother is very cross with me. And I know that you are too.' A breathless voice. Little girl innocent. So easy to accomplish. She leant over slightly so that the neckline of her day dress sagged open. 'He sent me here today to collect the chit that you so kindly offered us.'

If looks could kill, Caroline thought she might well be lying at his feet, and in truth the ridiculousness of the whole situation was beginning to hit home.

She had lied and he had exposed her. A hasty retreat might have been a better policy, yet in the face of their lack of finance even that was not a viable option.

'How much?' His words were clipped and as he leaned forward to take her hand she could not quite understand what it was that he meant.

'How much?' This time her voice sounded exactly like her own.

'How much are you paid for your services? With men?'

Shaken, she tried to disengage her hand, but he would not let her. She wondered if he felt the quick spark of shock as he touched her, jolting her into a breathless bewilderment. 'Oh,' she managed, 'I am not cheaply bought, Your Grace.'

'No?' The base of his first finger pressed down on her wrist, the blue vein marking the accelerated beat of blood. 'Is there a discount for the second time around?'

'You fun with me, sir. There was no first.'

'A pity you didn't relate that fact to the many interested ears of the *ton*.'

Uncertainty swamped her. 'I thought that you would not wish me to, for I had named you as the best of lovers by then and could not in all good faith take that sentiment back.'

'Why not?'

'Because it would have hurt you. Hurt your reputation.'

He dropped her hand and reached for the decanter of brandy on the table beside him, pouring out a liberal amount.

'Know that my reputation is the last thing I would worry about.'

'Then we have another thing in common, Your Grace.' She punctuated the unimportance of it all with a vacuous wave and rearranged her bounteous curls, but he ignored the sentiment and changed the subject completely.

'Where are your family, your people?'

'Thomas is my family,' she countered and accepted the brandy that he held out to her. The fluted glass was beautiful, she thought, as she raised it to her lips and drank, the warmth of the liquor bolstering confidence. It was not usual for a lady to drink brandy, especially at this time of day, but Caroline was not a conventional woman.

'Your parents?'

'Dead.'

'Your husband?'

'Killed.'

'And so your brother tries to make ends meet by plying the card tables and you try to help him by sleeping with whoever takes your interest?'

'He does and I do.' Fluttering her eyelashes, she pushed down a rising nervousness. A string of probing questions was the last thing she wanted, and she needed for him to see her as the shallow and flirtatious opportunist she portrayed.

'A rather uncertain profession, I should imagine, and dangerous. You seem young for it?'

'Young in years, but old in life.' She had read that line in a book once and had always wanted to use it. But it did not have quite the desired effect on Thornton Lindsay. Instead of being impressed, he laughed. Loudly.

'Why did you choose me as your would-be lover?'

Colouring, Caroline decided on honesty.

'I knew you to be a...recluse, a man who would not come to London to refute a small untruth. However, had I known of your injuries, I would have most certainly chosen another.'

'Because you feel sorry for me?' His deep voice sharpened, irritation easily audible.

'Sorry for you? I doubt you would allow that, Your Grace.'

He laughed again.

'How long have you been a courtesan?'

'Long enough.'

The gold in his one good eye darkened. Considerably.

'I will pay you fifty guineas to stay the night with me.' The words seemed dragged from his throat as if he could not quite control his voice and she looked up, startled.

'Fifty guineas?'

More money than she had ever held in all her life. Enough money to make a new start somewhere else. Excitement churned.

'Fifty guineas.' She repeated the figure just to make certain that she had heard rightly. And in that second Caroline saw the answer to their problems.

One night of shame in exchange for a new chance. No more scampering from town to town with the law on their heels and a weighty dollop of guilt on their shoulders.

'It cannot be tonight.'

His amber eye slanted in question.

'I am busy tonight,' she added and the meaning of her words flared in his face.

'Tomorrow night, then. Here. At six o'clock.'

Shoving his hands in his pockets he stood very, very still. When she nodded she could have sworn she saw relief.

'I shall expect you then, Miss Anstretton.'

Without waiting for her reply, he helped her into her coat and opened the door. A footman outside came forward and ushered her though to the hallway. When she turned to bid him goodbye, the library door was firmly shut.

Thornton replaced the lid on the brandy decanter and looked out on to the dreary day as he listened to the sounds of her carriage departing.

Why had he offered her such a bounty when, for an eighth of the price, he could have repaired to Venus's and used a girl with almost as much charm as that of Caroline Anstretton?

Almost.

It was in the touch of her fingers against his. And in the uncertainty of her eyes, the sooty lashes so long that when she looked down they rested on her cheeks. And her strange sense of honour.

She was a cheat and a liar and God knew what else. The reticule she carried had strained at the handles indicating something much heavier than just a handkerchief inside and the boots she wore were at least half a size too small.

She was making everything up.

He could feel it in every word she uttered. Questions! He smiled and turned to refill his glass.

His intelligence days were over and still they did not let him just be. Everyone was suspect; even a beautiful harlot who had made sure that her breasts had fallen easily into his line of vision and had accepted an assignation with very little pressure for tomorrow night.

Lord.

Tomorrow night and it had been years since he had had a woman.

The thought worried him.

'Lillyanna.' The softness of her name seemed like a travesty in the light of what he was about to do.

And yet in the remains of sorrow something else had suddenly budded and he could not just give it up.

Caroline Anstretton, with her rouged cheeks and breathless voice, had touched a part of him he had long thought of as dead.

A chance.

A chance to feel again?

Even at fifty guineas the exchange was cheap.

He called in his butler and instructed him to give the servants the next night off.

And then he pulled his pistol from a drawer and began to meticulously clean it.

Caroline laid her head against the padded cushioning of the coach she had rented. And breathed.

In and out.

Deeply.

Her hand shook as she pushed her red ringlets back against the lie of her shoulders and when she glanced outside she barely saw anything at all.

She had sold herself.

Sold herself to the first and highest bidder.

Sold herself for the price of freedom.

Sold herself to save her brother from spiralling downwards.

The brandy that had warmed her before now lay in a cold hard thickness at the bottom of her stomach and she shuffled on the seat. Her second-hand boots hurt her feet and the rock had begun to unravel the dainty stitches of silk on the bottom seam of her bag.

Unravelling.

Everything.

She could still be safe. She could simply not turn up tomorrow and leave London with her brother.

To go where? And with what? To Bath for a few days and when that welcome was up…?

Thornton Lindsay's money would afford them a passage out of London and the hope of the rent on a house until they could climb back upon their feet. She could sell portraits and her brother could work on the land. He had always liked the thought of growing his own food and fishing. Perhaps they could live by the sea.

Vegetables, a few chickens and the chance of a small boat. Caroline pictured a cottage, sitting high above a bay. Security. For a while.

All for the price of her virginity.

Lord. Her eyes flew open.

Her virginity?

Would he know?

Was it possible for a man not to know?

Her mother had said there would be blood and pain.

And if Tosh should ever find out? Taking a deep breath, she tried to devise a plan that would throw her brother off her trail.

Suzette.

Her friend had asked her to come and stay last week and Tosh had overheard the conversation.

Without waiting for another moment she ordered the driver to Clapham and asked him to wait whilst she ran just one simple errand.

What her brother did not know would not hurt him and his morals were ones that quite simply were no longer tenable. Not for her, set as she was outside of ever marrying well, her reputation tangled in disapproving threads of gossip.

One night and they could be on a carriage going west with a goodly sum of money in their pockets. And a new life.

A reasonable exchange.

If she could just get through tomorrow night.

Chapter Three

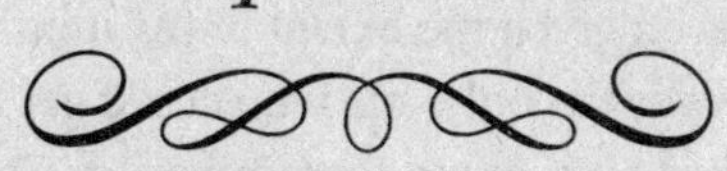

Caroline dressed carefully, her white muslin frock buttoned down the back and cinched up high just under her breasts. Today she had also worn a thick pelisse, the velvet coat knee-length and fur trimmed.

More for him to peel off, the voice in her head whispered as she turned to look at herself in the mirror.

A tasty sacrifice.

The rouge only highlighted the paleness of her face.

'Are you completely certain that this is the best of ideas, Caro? What if the Duke of Penborne tries to get you into his bed?'

She smiled. Wanly. 'He will not, Suzette. 'Tis just a dinner at his friend's house and a late concert.'

'Very late, if you ask me, seeing as you say you won't be home till the morning. Are you certain there is nothing you are not quite telling me, *chérie*?'

It was on the tip of her tongue to confess it all, but Caroline knew that, if she did that, there would be no way she could leave here with the certainty that her brother would not turn up at Lindsay House in the night and demand redress.

A duel.

At dawn and the Duke an accomplished shot by all accounts, even given the extent of his injuries.

No, she was the only one who could get them out of the mess they now found themselves in. Consequently she smiled and said nothing as she tied up her bonnet and stuffed her reticule with a hanky and a comb.

Two things for the night. She could not risk the inclusion of her nightgown in case Suzette saw it.

Massaging her right temple, she hoped that the pain would not worsen. Migraine or not, she was going through with this...business proposition. And if she could only half-see Thornton Lindsay, then all the better for it.

He opened the door himself when she knocked and straight away she could tell that he had been drinking. She could smell it on his breath when he reached forward and took her pelisse, the warmth of his fingers brushing her arms in a certain way.

When he closed the door behind her she felt as if she had strayed into a dream, as if she had passed through the threshold of good sense into some sort of unimaginable mistake.

'I thought that you would not come.'

'I am a woman of my word, Your Grace, and fifty guineas is a lot of money to turn down.'

'Indeed.'

His answer was closely whispered and tonight the scars on his face seemed less…frightening. The eye-patch he wore was made of soft leather, giving her the impression of the blinding of the falcons in centuries past that she had read about.

A falcon. That was exactly what he reminded her of. Alert. Dangerous. Vigilant. When his right hand reached out and touched her cheek she jumped back, her teeth biting into the soft inside of her mouth.

'You seem a little ruffled.'

'I had a late evening last night and I have a headache—'

He stopped her simply by placing the first finger of his right hand across her lips.

'As this assignment is affording you a large sum of money, I would appreciate you keep your mind upon the moment.'

Nodding, she met his eyes and frowned. No brutal lording glance stared back. Nay, today she saw only lust.

Such a simple word for what was next to happen.

'I hope you have ways of avoiding conception? A child is the last thing I would want from this union.'

'I have, Your Grace.' She fumbled for words and hated the aching fear at the back of her throat. What exactly did that mean? What were the ways that women ensured no child should come from a union?

'And you are cognisant of the fact that it is a whole night I have paid for.'

More than once? Many times? How many times?

Bought and sold.

The throbbing awareness she felt in her lower region surprised her. Lord. While her mind rebelled at such a life-changing act, her body melted into acquiescence. More than melted. She felt the heat as a blaze of pain, delved into the very marrow of her bones. And he had barely touched her…yet.

Her eyes went to the clock on the mantel. A quarter past six. Her innocence quivered beneath the heavier passing of time.

Still early.

Would he rip off her clothes and throw her on to the ottoman and have his way with her? She could not imagine how any of it would begin. When her breathing quickened, she felt the hard beat of blood in her throat and the thinner line of alarm in her stomach.

Thornton leant back against the wall and watched Caroline Anstretton eye up his ottoman. He knew apprehension when he saw it and hers was every bit as visible as that shining in the faces of the young and green boys he had so often consigned to battle.

But she was a courtesan and by all accounts a damn experienced one. And he was paying her well.

The light frock she wore disguised none of her abundant charms. Tightly draped about her body, it looked almost too...small, the generous curves easily seen, the swell of her breasts as visible as the wares in a shop window.

Her trading commodities.

The thought made him harden. He could take her whenever he wanted to and however he wanted to. After years of self-imposed celibacy, that realisation was a potent aphrodisiac.

He was glad that she had chosen white. It suited her. Suited his intentions. Virginal white to stave off the demons that raged inside him, aching for release.

Stepping forward, he cupped her elbow and pulled her closer. Here in the nearly dusk before the beeswax candles were lit, the shadows of late day masked their faces, any money paid for services mellowed beneath a kinder promise.

He could almost believe that she was Lillyanna resurrected from the dead. Warm. Alive. Laughing.

No. He could not have her like that and be healed.

He had to know that it was Caroline Anstretton. Vapid. Careless. For sale.

His fingers unbuttoned the cloth at her back and he was glad that she did not pull away or question. And her curves beneath the petticoat and chemise were enchanting.

'I want to see you.'

'Here, Your Grace?' She looked around the parlour and towards the door.

'I have dismissed my servants for the evening. They will not return until well into the morrow.'

She smiled, tremulously, and Thornton understood just exactly why it was said that she was the most beautiful woman to have ever come to London.

It was nothing to do with the red of her hair or the curls softly rounding her waist. Nothing to do with the alabaster skin strangely plied with a heavy layer of rouge. No, it was her eyes, the dark blueness of them studded in sparkle and dimples deeply etched into each cheek even when she did not smile.

'Would you possibly have some rum? I'd like it neat.' Her voice was low and beckoning.

Rum and neat! The drink of sailors and harlots and people who had little left to lose.

'Of course.' Stepping back, he poured her a double shot. She drank it quickly, draining even the few drops at the bottom of the glass before putting down her reticule and removing the bracelet at her wrist.

'I should not like to misplace this when we…if we…' Stopping, she laid the jewellery carefully on top of her bag, a dark flush of redness standing out on her cheeks.

'A bauble from an admirer, perhaps?' He did not know why he had asked that question given his blanket prohibition of the same subject a few moments prior, but he could not help himself. He was glad when she simply shook her head and turned to face him.

'Should I take my underclothes off?'

A blunt unpolished frankness that had him guessing that she had perhaps not been in this game as long as she had said. He frowned, the fright in her eyes making him soften his approach.

'I think we might eat first.'

Her laughter surprised him. A throaty laugh, the first real glimmer of the woman who was not a whore; because of it he ran his finger along the line of her jaw, tracing his way on to the smooth skin of her bottom lip.

Warm, wet, hot.

Like the rest of her?

The thick throb of desire almost unnerved him and he made himself slow down. The whole evening lay before them, after all, and he wanted to savour every damn moment of it.

Food! They would eat first? Relief rushed through Caroline, almost making her dizzy, and the rum compounded the whole effect. She rarely drank, apart from the occasional unconventional brandy, not even wine. But tonight with the thought of what she was about to do before her she could have picked up the whole bottle and emptied the contents down her throat. She was glad for the light silk shawl that he draped across her shoulders.

The table in the next room was set with numerous

candles and a fine supper. Pheasant and salmon, scallops of chicken and turbot, apricot tartlets and a compôte of apple. Fluted glasses completed the laying, the whole effect embellished by a large bowl of flowers sitting squarely in the middle of the cloth.

Thornton Lindsay pulled out a chair for her and was careful in his assistance. When he sat, the light caught his eye, amber velvet, and beneath the scars she could see again so easily the man he had once been.

Still was!

His frock coat was a dark, dark brown and he wore this over a charcoal waistcoat. And at his neck sat a simple white cravat. No pretence to the highest of fashion and it suited him, ornamentation and foppery a far cry from the interest of an officer who had caught the King's attention and favour after his bravery in Europe.

She longed to ask him about it all, about the battles and the intelligence work he was rumoured to have been so good at, but she stopped herself.

One night.

Anonymity.

And if she asked him questions, then he might ask them back of her. And she could not tell him anything. Nothing real, at least, for as a master of intelligence, she was certain that with only the least amount of information he could put together a whole tableau of possibility.

Consequently she lifted one fluted side plate and held the workmanship before a candle.

'Sèvres, is it not? I have always loved their designs.'

He did not answer.

'Once I went to a ball and the whole of the dinner set was embellished with white swans and I thought to myself, what if someone drops one, what if they should slip and...'

'Why did you need to name me as your lover?'

He broke into her diatribe, effortlessly, and his long fingers entwined round the crystal stem of his glass. One nail was blackened, she noticed, and the scars so evident on his other hand were harder to see on this one.

But still there, running up into the cuff of his snowy white shirt. The signet ring he wore was engraved with a crest that portrayed a knight's helm surrounded by roundlets. And half of his little finger was missing altogether.

'It was a mistake.' Frantically she plastered a smile on her lips and dropped her glance. What he could see on her face would not be reflected in her eyes and to make this whole charade work she needed him to believe in her story. 'My brother had thought he could best his opponent in a card game and when his coins ran out he bet me instead. Or my hand in marriage, rather. I remembered your name and used it.'

'And do you often partake in such...pranks?'

Gritting her teeth, she frowned and for just a second bleakness filled her. Filled her to the very ends of her toes. And she swallowed. Hard.

'Promise me you will return to England. Promise

me, Caroline. On your honour.' Her mother's voice as she lay dying on the edge of the winter of 1813. *'It is not safe here for you. Guy can be…'* She had stopped and tears had rolled down her cheeks.

A bully? A pervert? An intimidating oppressive tyrant. She had been seventeen and no match for him. Until Tosh had saved her!

Shaking her head at the memory, she steeled herself to her set task.

'I am a woman of the night, Your Grace.' Licking her lips, she helped herself to a goodly proportion of the turbot in a lobster sauce.

'Delicious,' she proclaimed after trying a little piece, the fish sticking in her throat like cardboard.

Anything to get your mind off me and on to the food, her subconscious screamed.

But he did not eat, did not even pick at the grapes on a plate next to his elbow. Rather he watched her. Closely.

'I have heard it said that you lived in Paris?'

She took her time before nodding. 'I spent some time there a few years ago?'

Beat. Beat. Beat. Her heart in her ears and danger.

In consternation she reached for the wine glass, clumsily, and it toppled over and over and over, the red staining white linen and blossoming like a pool of blood, almost transparent at the edges.

He was not a man to be trifled with. Even from here

she could see his brain ticking over, a plethora of facts evident in the keen perception of his one uncovered eye.

Suddenly she just wanted the whole thing to be over. Completed. The money in hand. Finished.

Fifty guineas of freedom.

With care she pushed her arms in close against her sides, the shawl falling away and the flesh of her breasts swelling markedly.

When his gaze thickened, she knew that she had him.

Thornton put down his wine glass and stood. Any thought of food flew out of the window as the bounty of her womanhood was so carelessly offered. Giving her his hand, he pulled her up.

She smelt of roses and softness, and her hair tickled the side of his cheek.

It had been so long since he had had a woman. So long since he had touched another person with…care.

He ran his finger down the length of her bare arm and slipped the material on her chemise lower. Her nipple stood proud in the cold and he forced up her eyes to his to make sure that she knew where it was he was looking.

'I want you. Now.'

When she nodded he simply bent his head and suckled, the taste of sweetness and the brighter echo of a time in his life when everything had been easy and innocent. A time when he had not known how to break a man's neck or leave a family in tatters simply because politics demanded tough choices and he was the only one left alive to make them.

Lillyanna.

He shook away memory.

Caroline. The soft easy abundance of her charms and the husky cadence of her voice. Alive. Real. Here. When he looked up again, the heavy languid burn of sex showed in the shadows of her eyes and in the pull of her hand against his.

And when she traced the outline of her lips with the tip of her tongue he leant forward.

To take.

Apprehension exited Caroline's body in a single second to be replaced by liquid silver longing, and delight. It was not hurt he had paid for after all.

She felt his tongue lave the surface of her breast and the sharp sting of pressure when he nipped her. Not hard. Not hard enough. Her fingers threaded through the darkness of his hair, drawing him in closer, pressing outwards, filling his mouth and her body, and making them one. An unbidden groan. Hers. More it said, *and more*.

And when he shifted focus to lifting the thin muslin petticoat she opened her legs further and invited him in. Needing, craving, everything. With her head tipped back and her neck stretched tight against the raw desperateness of want, she felt as if she was floating. Weightless.

Waiting. His fingers weaving a magic that she had never believed could be possible.

'Now?'

Had he heard her?

No more hesitation.

When he led her into the parlour again she did as he bid and lay down on the thick rug, watching as he removed his jacket and waistcoat. The clock against the mantel chimed seven and the day outside deepened into night. One night.

This night. The money on the table beside her bag.

Fifty shining guineas.

Payment.

Her hand reached into the material beneath his shirt as he lay across her. Scars and knotted skin. The essence of him. Strength and steel. Tempered with gentleness. The soap he used left an elusive scent and when she caressed his chest, as he had done to hers, she heard him take in breath and was pleased. The corded knots of muscle in his throat stilled and the heavy beat of his heart quickened. And further down she felt the hardening of his sex laid long against her stomach. Ready.

More than ready.

His finger slipped inside her, testing. She was tight, moist.

When her knees fell open she heard the rent of lawn. Exposed. Bare. The swell of her stomach white with moonlight.

Waiting to be taken.

The thought egged her on, made her hips buck up into his hands, asking for something she knew nothing about.

Then he was in her, stopping, retreating, before the hilt of his manhood slipped home into the warm darkness of her very being.

'God, you are so tight.'

Thornton tried to stay still, tried to stop the wrenching waves of climax that beached themselves in the very act of caution. And then he was lost. Lost to this world as he spilled his seed into her. Without protection. Without anything. On and on and on until the red blazing lust was sated and he had no more breath to even lift himself off her. Covering. Her white against his brown, spread against the night. The musky smell of what was between them filling the air. Finished. Satisfied. Undone. The slash of her red full lips smudged against the moment.

Tears? He felt them warm against his chest. And felt them again in the uneven gait of her breathing.

Instantly he lifted himself away from her, feeling for the tinderbox.

'No.' She stopped him with her hand. 'Just the moonlight.'

'If I hurt you…'

'You did not.'

She sat up and tried to bring the fabric of her petticoat together. 'I brought no other clothes with me…'

The clock chimed the half-hour. Loudly. Surprising them both.

'Will it be safe?' His question. As if now that they had been joined he could read her mind.

'I think it will be so.'

The expletive told her that her answer was not the one he was after. When his hand stilled she knew what he was about to say and stopped him.

'No, I shall not be with child. A woman of my persuasion has other ways of making certain.'

Other ways? For fifty guineas she would find a way—she did not want irritation to change his mind about the amount.

His fingers tightened around her upper arm; bringing her on to his lap, he tilted her hips and claimed her breasts.

One night. All night. The clouds and the moon and the darkness rolled into one and the clenching want made her shake, made her sweat, made her say his name in the wildness of passion.

'Thornton?'

Just as a question.

And then she could say nothing.

Much later he took her upstairs to his bedroom, the quiet light of candles suiting his purpose of truly seeing her body as he stripped off her chemise and petticoat and waited for her to wake up.

Two o'clock. Four hours before daybreak and the end of a bargain.

Too soon. He willed the hours to travel more slowly and bent to wake her.

The touch of a finger against her cheek, a gentle finger, his finger. Her hand came up to cup his, and he saw a crescent-shaped scar on her thumb as she pushed forward.

Kiss me, she longed to ask.

For he had not kissed her once.

Not even when she had taken his face and brought it up to her own.

The truth hit her suddenly. Men did not kiss courtesans. She had heard that bit of news from her brother when he had returned home from an evening with his wilder friends.

Did not kiss.

Did not kiss.

She was surprised by the loss she felt at this knowledge.

The wallpaper in the room also surprised her. They were no longer in the parlour. This room was larger, more elaborate. The softness of mattress beneath her and above the canopied bed, draped in burgundy velvet held open by tassels of multi-coloured silk. A full-length mirror to one side of the bed caught the flame of candles burning on silver plinths.

Turning, she caught him looking at her, and was astonished to see that he had removed his eye patch. No scars were visible.

With care she traced her finger across his brow and, heartened by his smile, asked her question.

'I thought there must be some disfigurement?'

'No.' He returned gently. 'It just gets tired sometimes.'

'What happened?'

'I was not careful enough.'

Catching her hand, he brought her forefinger into his mouth when she went to say more. Sucking. Warm.

'No past, all right. Just now. Just tonight.'

She understood and, emboldened by his words, wrapped her leg around his, pleased when he rolled on top of her. Her breasts were squeezed beneath the heaviness of his body and he caught at her hands, dragging a long silk tassel to bind her wrists to the bed-head and tying off the knot with his mouth. And one arm came beneath her hips, raising them and pressing open her legs.

'This time I will watch you,' he said simply, and trailed his fingers up the insides of her thighs, up and up to the fullness of them, touching a place high within her, a place where the thin pain of delight blossomed and grew, the throb of the nearly-there elusive until the bolster of his arm beneath her tightened and the clenching contractions tugged at reason. She called his name loud, loud, loud in the night, slicked in the smell of him, tight-close bound, the movement of his fingers beginning again even as the last orgasms were fading.

Heaven.

She never wanted to leave this room, his magic had woven her fear and need into something else indescribable.

Love?

The word came unbidden and she squashed it back, the fifty guineas decrying such a promise.

And then she forgot to think altogether.

She sat on the bed after eight in the morning and rolled up her stockings, every part of her body vibrating with a languid heat as he watched her from across the room.

She wanted another night. Another thousand nights!

Her stockings, dress and pelisse were all she had left, her underclothes balled in a broken ruin.

He had mentioned no further contact. He had not asked her for anything.

Just this night.

No past.

No future.

Finished.

Filled.

Banished.

When he buttoned her coat about her she was silent. When he told her he had hailed a carriage to the door to take her home she did not look at him. And when he pushed the money into her hands she did not thank him.

* * *

The coach ride home to Suzette's was like a dream and Caroline was glad to find the house empty when she let herself in.

Once inside, she peeled off her clothes and washed. Washed the scent of him from her body and the feel of him from her limbs. Placed lavender oil where pure masculine strength had left the marks of loving and massaged attar of roses through her hair, now bereft of the wig.

Much later she sat bound in a bath cloth before a mirror and allowed herself to truly look into the depths of her eyes.

Enchantment sparkled.

And disbelief.

And nowhere lingered shame or reproach.

Unexpected. Freeing.

She had been brought into the delights of womanhood by a master, and regretted none of it.

When the tears came they were not filled with sorrow for what she had done. No, they were filled with the secret aching anguish of knowing that such a night would never happen again, and that any knowledge of another man would be tempered by this one unattainable perfection—Thornton Lindsay.

Even now his golden eyes watched her in memory,

etched in sadness and hurt, lust measured only in the hours of payment.

Balling her fists, she pushed away the sweet promise of impossibility and began to dress for her journey home.

Chapter Four

'So you are telling me that the Duke of Penborne gave you fifty guineas just like that. I don't believe you.'

Tosh was as furious as Caroline had ever seen him and she struggled to find words to placate the anger. She had never lied successfully to his face and wasn't about to start now.

'Well, it wasn't quite like that.'

'You bedded him, didn't you? You tupped the bastard for money.'

'No, I slept with him because every single part of my body wanted to know what it would be like to make love to Thornton Lindsay and for the first time ever I felt…I felt whole.' Swiping away the gathering tears from her face, she kept going. 'It wasn't dirty or rough or hurting, it was just…beautiful.'

'Lord.' Her brother's anger foundered the second he

saw her tears and he moved forward, his arms coming around her and holding her close. 'Lord,' he repeated. 'So where exactly does this leave us now?'

'With a passage from London and the means to survive for at least another year if we are very careful.'

'I wasn't talking about our future, Caro. I was thinking more about yours and Lindsay's.'

'There is no future. He made that clear.'

'And if you are with child?'

She was silent.

'I see. And if you meet him again?'

'I won't. The money will allow us passage to wherever we want to go, Tosh. A leeway for a while at least…'

Shaking his head he sat down on the chair. Dazed.

'At what cost, Caroline?'

'At the cost of twelve hours of pure delight, Thomas.'

Puzzlement etched his features, and also a good measure of relief. 'Then you do not wish for me to call on him?'

'And say what? Insist that he marry me and challenge him to a duel when he refuses. He is said to be one of the finest shots in all of England, even given his injuries, and what indeed would you be fighting for? My reputation?' She shook her head. 'My God, that disappeared the moment we left Paris. No, far better to take the money and simply disappear. Become other people and start again.'

'So you are not…hurt in any way because of this?'

Disquiet surfaced at her brother's perception.

'He gave no mention of seeing me again. He wanted no further contact.' A single tear slipped down her cheek and she wiped it away with the back of her hand.

'If we went to his town house together, Caro, and told him a part of our story…'

'Which part? The part about murdering our mother's lover and being in disguise ever since?'

'I was thinking more about the part where he should take some responsibility for what he has done. You are not a courtesan and he used you as one. If he knew who you truly were, then perhaps he would—'

She didn't let him finish.

'I never want him to know that. Never.'

'Why?'

'Because if he offered marriage under duress….'

'You like him, damn it. You do. I can see it in your eyes and hear it in your words.'

Caroline turned away. She had had enough of supposition and wanted to be far away from London, far away from Thornton Lindsay, far away from the temptation of just turning up on his doorstep again and offering him another night.

And another one.

She was pleased when Thomas brought out their battered old map of England and laid it on the table between them.

'Your turn to pick a place this time, Caro.'

She simply closed her eyes and laid her finger on the

paper and when she opened them the name of Mortehoe was easily read.

On the coast, near Barnstaple, the gentle shores of the Bristol Channel lapping at its feet. A new beginning. And this time she resolved to be a widow. A very prim and proper widow who would make it clear from the beginning that the husband she had lost was her very first and definitely very last love.

Thornton held the remains of her petticoat in his hands, the delicate white lawn somehow symptomatic of Caroline Anstretton, though flecks of blood made him pause. Had he hurt her somehow, or was it his own, a result of her nails as they had raked hard down his back in the final act of taking?

She had been nothing at all as he had expected. An experienced courtesan with all the wiles of a virgin? He laughed. She had been married once and had had her fair share of lovers. Perhaps acting the *ingénue* was the way that she had thought he had wanted her to play it, and fifty guineas was a lot of money in anyone's book.

The gold bracelet on the floor caught him by surprise. She had forgotten it after being so careful to remove it in the first place. He lifted it up and in the light of the day an inscription showed on the middle band.

Paris 1807—TStC.

A bracelet fashioned not in England, but in France? He held the delicate chain in the middle of his palm and looked more closely at it. The emeralds encrusted in the middle were all fake and the metal was thin, brittle and cheap. Almost the jewellery a child might treasure and a strange thing for a courtesan to value so highly?

Perhaps she was down on her luck. Perhaps that was why she had named him as her lover in the first place.

Questions.

Puzzles.

And an indefinable interest.

She had got to him with her strange mix of innocence and naïve righteousness, and when he had felt the soft touch of her lips on his cheek he had almost been undone.

Almost.

Placing the bracelet on the table and his hands in his pockets, he closed his eyes and listened to the sounds outside. A passing carriage, the wind in the trees, the sounds of birds on the shrubs by the front windows, the footsteps of pedestrians going about their business.

For so long the sounds of life around him had been measured, deciphered, collated, interpreted; the smallest of noises a warning against an enemy that had never slept. And suddenly, now, today, this second, he felt unreasonably tired by it all.

He wanted a normal life, a real life, a life that included sitting in a room without his back to the wall and a well-weighted blade in the deep pockets of his jacket. A life without the brutal aching regret of war and the suffocating fear of loneliness that had consumed him since coming home. A life with a woman to warm his bed and his nights, a woman to make him laugh again and feel again and touch his ruined cheek with the same care as Caroline Anstretton had.

A wife?

Perhaps that was what he needed! A happy sunny-natured girl who was as open-minded as he was closed and who had never once in all of her life knowingly told a lie.

Not a paragon.

He did not want that, but virtue had its own ease and was a cosy companion when the demons raging inside of him threatened to take over. After all, he was wealthy and passably young, and the half of his face that he had left was not unpleasant.

She would not be Lillyanna. He knew that. But Caroline Anstretton had shown him something that he would have never thought possible even as recently as last night.

The feel of soft skin against his hand, the warmth of her against his back, the smell of roses and woman. His blood had risen, easily, hard grief softened beneath the promise of the forgotten, and coursing through his body like a river in winter after the rains, all the banks washed away under the onslaught of an unexpected and startling thawing.

Even now in broad daylight he could still feel the sharp echoes of his body's response, and he smiled.

If he offered her the position of his mistress whilst he searched for the new Duchess of Penborne, he could kill two birds with one stone. His lust and her need for money, and a companionship that would be beneficial to the both of them.

Taking a fresh sheet of paper from his armoire, he dipped his quill in ink. A careful offer, quartered in the temporary. She was a courtesan and he was a duke. It was, quite honestly, all that she could expect.

At three in the afternoon when the doorbell rang, Thornton sat up and listened with interest as he made out the voice of his visitor.

Caroline Anstretton. Here in person to answer the generous terms of his offer? It took all his resolve to make himself stay in his seat behind his desk and wait.

She was wearing a heavy wool jacket over a yellow gown and her hat sat across carefully arranged red curls. In her hand he saw his letter, her fingers clutching the sheet in a way that made him cautious.

'Your Grace.' She curtsied and waited till his man departed and the look in her eyes was disconcerting. Knowing. Flaunting.

Something had changed. He could feel it in the air between them and in the space of silence that last night would have been filled with anticipation. Today a wooden awkwardness replaced ease and her fingers shook as she deposited his note on the table.

'I think perhaps you may have got the wrong impression of me last night.'

'Impression?' He frowned when she did not quite look at him.

'I am not a woman who could possibly...ever...be with just one man. Not like that, you understand.' Gesturing to his letter, she continued. 'The position you offer of mistress, whilst flattering and indeed very generous in its terms, is rather a restricting sort of arrangement. For me.'

'You are saying you would want more,' he returned, the hint of anger in his voice annoying him.

'Well, Your Grace, I am young...and many say I am the most beautiful woman to have come to London in... years and years.' She turned to the mirror above the mantel and moved her head this way and that.

Admiring herself!

'Perhaps it is in the line of my jaw or the colour of my eyes or the way my nose tilts just here.'

Puzzlement gave way to plain distaste.

'Why, I have already had an offer for my hand in marriage, from a lord, no less, and the family is not at all daunted by my reputation. But my brother thinks I should wait a while and hope for better.' When she giggled, the brittle vacuous sound rankled.

She was vain and stupid.

He had not expected that.

'It's not that I don't like you, you understand. Last night was wonderful, it's just—' He didn't let her finish.

'It's just that you would rather be a duchess than a mistress.'

'Exactly.' Her blue eyes widened and she shook her abundant red curls, hopefully he thought, as he made himself smile.

'I shall remember your offer, Miss Anstretton. But as I am returning to Cornwall tomorrow, I shall decline it.'

'Oh.' She made a lot of ironing out the folds of her skirt, the yellow of the fabric bright against the paleness of the skin on her hand. All her nails were short.

Flipping open a drawer, he extricated her bracelet. 'You left this here last night and, as it seemed important, I would like to return it to you.'

Sharp relief filled her eyes as she fastened the catch around her wrist, testing it by shaking her hand.

'Thank you.' For the first time today a small shiver of what had been between them last night returned and her bottom lip quivered. If she had looked at him then, he might have reached out, requesting explanation, but her quick movement away demanded silence. When she raised the reticule from the seat where she had flung it on first entering the room, he knew that he had lost her.

'I have a fitting for a new gown in half an hour. Madame Celeste has chosen it for me and I shall wear it first to the Forsythe ball in Kent in a month. Perhaps if you return unexpectedly from your home in the country, you could look me up and be my partner. For old times' sake.'

When he did not answer she held out her hand, giving Thornton no option but to take it. The coldness of her fingers was startling. Yesterday she had been like a living flame. He dropped it immediately.

'I do not like to dance.'

Her eyes flicked to his left leg as she answered, 'No, of course not, I am sorry…'

Embarrassment and pity were written across her face and all he wanted was for her to go.

But she did not. Not until she had leaned forward and touched his left cheek, softly, her thumb running on across his bottom lip.

And then she was gone, the lingering scent of her perfume all that was left in the silence.

'Lord.' Thornton filled his brandy glass and downed the contents in one shot, the touch of her hand still burning.

'Lord,' he repeated and leant back against the wall. His instincts about people were usually well honed and seldom wrong, but Caroline Anstretton confused him.

A conceited harlot or a brilliant actress—there was something in her story that did not quite add up. Something in the way she had clung to him last night, an edge of unsullied innocence in her lovemaking.

She would not be a mistress and yet she would be a wife! Even *his* wife, should he up the stakes and offer her his hand. He smiled, for something in him even wanted to throw caution to the wind and take a chance, take a punt on last night's loving returning again, and take her with him to Penleven. To safety.

But he could not quite do it.

Not till he knew a lot more about her, about them, the brother and sister who had come to London out of nowhere and created such a storm.

His head began to ache against the complexity of it all and he poured himself a large glass of water. London and its business bore down upon him in a way the countryside around Penleven never did, making him remember things he would far rather have forgotten.

Lilly there with him in the happy times before she had died at Orthez, in the south-west of France, blown into pieces during the last defensive campaign of Napoleon. His regiment had been assigned to the town and when the French four-pounders had battered their position they had taken refuge in a small stone church that, in retrospect, had made an easy target. Twenty men and Lilly, and very few of them had come out alive. Just another assignment that had ended her life and changed his and nothing had been the same since.

Hating the alarm that was beginning to pool across his forehead and the numbness that was overtaking his hands, he pressed his thumbs against his temple. Memories were closer here. All encompassing. And the injuries that had left him temporarily blinded still bore down upon his health two years later.

'Lillyanna,' he called as she came towards him, her skirt billowing blue and laughter in her eyes.

'Lillyanna,' he shouted as the roof caved in. Red

rolling pain and slow, slow movement. And fabric floating downwards, all that was left of joy and goodness.

And when the shaking started he let go of the wall and felt himself fall, hard against the floor, sweat-slicked and hot, the sins of his past weighing against his chest and denying him breath.

The light made him open his eyes. Bright. Too bright. Holding up his hand, he tried to shield his face from it.

His butler Henry was in the room. And his secretary James. Their faces an exact copy of each other's.

'How long this time?'

'Twelve hours, Your Grace.'

He shut his eyes. Twelve hours? Last time it had been only a few. An improvement or a decline? He liked the land of limbo that he had been consigned to, forgetful drowsiness and the absence of memory, but if he did not return…?

'Is there water?' His words sounded thick, skewered.

Henry poured him a glass from a jug on the bedside table, lifting his head. One sip and then two. A sheen of perspiration and nausea. He winced and tried to concentrate on what James was saying.

'François de Gennes was here this morning and left word that he will return again on the morrow. In the afternoon.'

The name hit Thornton with an ache.

Lillyanna's brother. He had had no contact at all with

François in three years, but knew instinctively what he was after.

Names.

The claws of intelligence sharpened against the futility of an oath sworn when he was twenty. Sometimes it seemed like a lifetime ago, a green boy with the naïve hope burning in his heart of making the world a better place.

Better for whom?

Not for himself.

Not for Lillyanna.

Not for the people he had killed, slung into unmarked graves on the edge of a conflict few of them truly understood.

And now François was here? In London.

Thornton wanted to be home—home with the noise of the sea against Lizard Point and the lonely call of gulls as they wheeled above the cliffs before heading seawards.

Sanctuary.

Sparkling blue eyes distracted his musings and he wondered again what Caroline Anstretton was doing at this exact moment.

Flirting, probably. Or angling for the hand of a titled peer who had no notion of the deceit that underlined such beauty, her ivory skin hot as she leaned towards him.

Shaking his head, he finished off a glass of water.

'Leave her to it,' he whispered beneath his breath, angry that she should even be taking up a moment more of his time.

* * *

François returned the next morning. His hair was a shade lighter and the lines around his eyes had deepened and Thornton noticed a long weal of raised skin along the line of his knuckles.

François caught him looking and smiled.

'The peace of the past year has not been as easy as I hoped. You, on the other hand, seem much recovered. Lilly would be pleased.'

The mention of his sister made Thornton frown. Connections and favours. He waited to see what was to come next, resolutely ignoring his headache.

'I have recently come into the possession of a note written to Lillyanna the day before she was killed. It was unsigned.' Reaching into his jacket pocket he extracted an envelope. 'If you took a look, I thought you perhaps might recollect...something, anything.'

Reluctantly Thornton took the letter. As he glanced at the handwriting, he stiffened in shock.

'Adele Halstead wrote this. I recognise the handwriting.'

'Wroxham's wife?'

'She was one of our sleepers in the Peninsular Campaign. I saw her correspondence many times.'

'Did her husband know?'

'I am not sure. I only found out her identity by mistake when the carrier let it slip he had come from the "Mistress of Wroxham".'

Thorn read the gist of the message and anger crystallised.

A specific warning. Why had Lilly not taken the caution to heart and stayed away from the little town outside Orthez? Why had she not, at least, warned him? And how was it that Adele Halstead should have been cognisant of any French army movements in the first place? A growing sense of betrayal made him wary. 'I think it might be wise to pay a visit to the Halsteads.'

Folding the paper, he carefully gave it back and did not question the look of relief in his old friend's eyes.

Chapter Five

There was no moon, not even a sign of one hanging on the horizon as they tethered their horses in front of the Wroxham town house.

Ten o'clock. He hoped that Adele Halstead would be at home as he had received no reply to the note sent earlier in the day, requesting a meeting.

François slid in against him and looked up at the rain filled sky. 'The weather is turning, Thorn. Do you think they will have company?'

'I am not certain.' He pulled a knife from his belt and tucked it into the folds of his sleeve. Out of sight. François looked perturbed.

'She is a woman. You would not kill her…'

'It is 1816, Franc, and peace is upon us.'

'Uneasily.'

Thorn laughed and knocked on the door, surprised

when a rather weary-looking butler answered almost immediately. 'Can I help you, sir? Sirs,' he amended as he caught sight of François.

Thornton pulled a card from his pocket and handed it over to the man. 'We have come to see Lady Adele.'

The man frowned. 'I am sorry, Your Grace, but she and her husband left this morning for her sister's house in Kent and shall not be returning 'til the morrow. I would be happy, however, to forward your card into her hands when she returns.'

'I see.' He moved back, feeling a vague sense of unease, the shadows of trees in the mounting wind jogging memories of other nights in other towns. Something was not quite right. He felt it in the air as he looked around and saw a shadowy figure signalling from the roofline in a brief slant of moonlight.

Ordering François to stay outside, Thornton charged up to the door again and rapped hard. When the same servant answered he pushed him aside and strode in.

'I think you have intruders in the house. What are the rooms facing the street on the second storey?'

'My mistress's rooms, sir.' The tiredness had vanished and he looked relieved when Thorn bade him to remain at the bottom of the staircase. Civilians were more trouble than they were worth in times of struggle and this servant was decidedly frail.

A fire was dying back in the grate of the chamber as he slipped inside and stopped, waiting for his eyes to acclimatise to an even darker space. The smell of the town house seeped in around him, damp, old and unkempt.

A tabby cat slumbered on the chair, its pupils gleaming in the small light of the embers and a clock boomed the hour of ten loudly from further out.

On instinct he checked his own timepiece. Ten past. Running slow. Everything about this place seemed lost in time.

Every chamber he checked was empty. He determined this quickly, though a noise outside one window made him pause. A soft scrape of boots against the slate of the roof and a heavier bang before silence reigned again. But not for long!

A head poked around the window frame and then a leg hooked across the sill with some skill as the interloper gained traction. A lad with a hat tucked low across his head.

Thornton waited as the newcomer came further into the room, tripping on the upturned corner of a thick Aubusson rug.

'Damn. Damn. Damn.' A distinct whispered curse before a hand-held candle lightened the room. In the beam he picked out a dirty face, teeth worrying the bottom lip in a peculiarly feminine movement.

Removing a drawer, the interloper emptied the contents across the coverlet of the bed, turning out the second and third drawers when the first proved fruitless. Thornton knew the exact second that he found what it was he sought. A whistle distracted him after a few seconds had passed.

Someone else was close. He watched as the lad walked to the window and waved his candle three times before blowing it out.

A signal.

Of success?

Stepping into the pale light, Thornton crossed the room and the lad turned in fright.

'If you make a sound, I will kill you. Understand?'

A short nod and then stillness.

It was difficult to make out any features, though the shaking of his bottom lip was clearly visible.

A newly commissioned thief. A green and timid pilferer with neither weapon nor sense.

'Keep still and raise your arms.' His firm command brought on a rush of words.

'I'm not here to hurt anyone, guv, it's just some money I need to help me mum and the little ones.'

A young voice, tremulous, rough and familiar, even given the thick cockney accent. He frowned, for the accent did not quite ring true, the lilt at the end of each sentence and intonation somehow…unEnglish. Memory of other times flooded back, for his wanderings on the continent had brought him into contact with many a man wanting to hide his true identity and choosing to speak instead with the voice of another.

Like this one did.

'How old are you, lad?'

'Thirteen, sir. I be fourteen next month.'

'Old enough to know the insides of a jail, then?'

'Please, sir, I'd never hurt no one, and me mum's hungry and me dad is gone—'

'Enough.'

'I'm all that she's got left, guv…'

The voice petered out as Thorn frowned.

A slight scent had caught his attention. Roses. Not the usual odour that one associated with young boys. Caroline Anstretton had smelled exactly the same the other night as he had stripped off her dress.

Shaking his head, he wondered if the tryst had driven sense from it. Lord, all he could think of was the softness of her skin and the feel of her body beneath his. Even here in the bedchamber of an enemy and in the company of a thief? With more force than he meant to, he pushed the lad down on to the side of the bed and lifted the candle. His tinder was dry and it took less than two seconds for the flame to take. Light made the room bigger and he saw that the youth was shaking, tightly drawn-in lips the only thing genuinely determined in a grubby visage.

'What was it you were wanting here?'

When the boy did not answer him, he emptied the right-hand pocket of his trousers in one short movement and took in a breath.

Not gold or jewels at all but a locket, a bauble worth only a fraction of nearly every other thing in the room.

He revised his opinion of the youth being a thief. Nay, there was another motive, he was sure; flicking the locket open, he had his answer.

Thomas Anstretton's face was younger and happier, but the mouth and eyes were exactly the same.

And before he even looked at the other side he knew the sister's face would grace it.

'Who the hell are you?'

Danger spiralled. He was too old and jaded to believe in the coincidence of chance.

The lad rose from the bed and tried to snatch back the locket; as he did so the chain of a familiar bracelet appeared from beneath the folds of a too-big shirt.

Lord.

Suddenly Thornton knew exactly who this was. Knew it to the very marrow of his bones. Neither a lad nor a cockney, but a courtesan and a liar.

Ripping off the hat, he was surprised again. No long red tresses tumbled down to her waist. Instead, unruly short blonde curls sprouted, curls threaded in gold and wheat and white honey, the deep sparkling blue of her eyes highlighted by the colour.

'You.'

Nothing made sense. Secrets beneath secrets and the first glimmer of something more sinister.

Adele Halstead, Lillyanna and the Anstretton twins tangled in a web of deceit and subterfuge. No simple burglary this, but a carefully targeted hit.

'I can explain if you would just let me...'

'Please do.' His civility was barely measured.

'The locket is ours. Lady Wroxham stole it from my mother. You can ask her. This is not a theft.' Her sentences were cut short by fear and breathlessness.

'And why should she want it?'

'She hates us. Hates who we are.'

Suddenly it all made sense. 'Because you are Halstead's mistress?'

This time he was certain of the emotion shining forth in her eyes. Pain and hurt and perplexity.

'You think I would sleep with him?'

'He is an earl,' he reminded her. 'I thought you were angling up the ranks of the peerage. And Wroxham is well moneyed.'

'He already has a wife.' Her argument cut through logic, but as he went to say more a noise from behind made him turn and the dull thud of something crossed his temple. Stars blossomed as he made one last flailing attempt to grab his assailant before the world lost shape.

A sharp curse and the soft feel of her fingers against his face, then all he knew was darkness.

Caroline watched Thomas replace the pistol in the belt of his trousers and bent to feel for a pulse at Thornton Lindsay's throat.

'You hit him too hard, damn it,' she growled, though the steady beat reassured her. As relief surged she stroked back a wayward curl that had crossed his forehead.

How much did he know about them?

Straightening out his fingers, she collected the locket, the thin white scars that covered his hands taking her back to another time, a time when he had run them across the naked skin between her thighs, searching, wanting.

A pure bolt of passion tripped across the core of her being, startling her with its intensity.

Why would he be here in Adele Halstead's room, knife in hand and the look of the haunted in his eyes? Had he still some connection with her through his intelligence work? She knew the answer as soon as she formulated it.

Lillyanna de Gennes.

The woman who had died in the church outside Orthez.

Shock intertwined with horror.

Lillyanna. Running. Towards Thornton Lindsay and his group of soldiers.

She began to shake as the possibility of exposure became real. His scars. His involvement in espionage.

They had heard later as they had crossed into Spain that one British soldier pulled from the wreckage of the chapel had called out the name of his lover.

Lillyanna.

The world began to close in on her though she was shaken back to reality by her brother's whisper, filled with worry.

'We need to go, Caro, before he awakens and there is less than ten hours to catch the early coach to Bristol.'

'I know.' She did not want to stand and go, to leave him like this, not conscious, vulnerable, the darkness of deceit hanging across the room like a pall.

But there was nothing else to do.

Pushing her forefinger to her lips, she transferred the kiss to his. *'J'espère vous revoir bientôt,'* she whispered before stepping from the room behind her brother and out into the night. *I look forward to seeing you again.*

'I don't think you should be drinking.'

Thornton smiled and took another swig of the brandy from his flask as he looked up at François.

His head still swam and the realisation of Caroline Anstretton's deception made the throbbing worse.

Lord, he had been one of Wellington's masters of intelligence during the Peninsular Campaign and here he was, being duped by a girl whose persona changed every time he met her. And changed markedly.

Who the hell was she and where was she now?

'Who hit you?' François's hands were steady as he checked the gash on the back of his head. Fire consumed agony as he pressed down on the wound. All around them stood a ring of the Wroxham servants, eyes wide open at such an unexpected happening.

'I don't know.' Lifting up his flask, Thorn clung to

the cold of it. Why was he lying? Why would he even think to protect her?

He knew everything about Caroline Anstretton that she was not. Not a thief. Not a redhead. Not English.

If she kept up this subterfuge, she would soon run into the hands of someone who would hurt her. Badly.

But how could he find her? Where could he look? The systems of intelligence that had at one time surrounded him were no longer in place. He felt in his jacket and was not surprised to find the locket missing.

Tilting his head, he tried to remember the intricate design on the outside of the casing. It had been dark and he had glanced at the bauble for only a second. Concentrating, he went backwards. The smell, the light, the shapes and sounds. Think. Remember. Basic rules of espionage surfaced as he searched for a pathway and the same silent awareness that had kept him in such good stead for six long winters in France surfaced.

Little clues. Reminders. The feel of her skin against his and the smell of roses.

There is less than eight hours to catch the early coach to Bristol. Hearing was always the last of the senses to dim.

Grappling for his timepiece, he saw that it was almost eleven.

'Get the horses, Franc.'

Ignoring the headache and the protests of his friend, Thornton pulled himself up, stopping for a moment as the dizzy whirl of pain made him feel ill. He had to find out exactly who Caroline Anstretton was and understand the strange connection that kept throwing her up into his life.

In his experience, chance always led to trouble and the presence of Adele Halstead worried him even more.

The answer lay in the bauble, he was sure of it, not in its worth, which was negligible, or in the likenesses of the Anstretton twins inside, but in the reason it was hidden in the first place.

Caro saw him from a distance. He sat on his horse with a companion beside him, both watching the steady stream of patrons stepping up to the Bristol coach. Pulling into the shadows of a side street, she gestured for Thomas to wait, her brother seeing them a second after she had. 'Damn, I thought I hit him hard enough to keep him out of action for at least a week.' His voice was filled with an undercurrent of respect. 'And how the hell could he have known we would be here?'

'I think we spoke of these plans when he was unconscious.'

'And he heard? Perhaps the things they say of him are true after all.'

Both turned back to look at him. The morning mist was rising as Lindsay drew his collar up against the cold, and, with his eyepatch and soldier's hat, those around gave him a wide leeway. A constant reminder of difference, Caroline thought, and hoped futilely that he would not notice, would not see the way onlookers glanced away from the spectre of such horrific injuries. Still, with the promise of leaving London close, her spirits rose. She had the locket and fifty guineas burning in her pocket. She had Tosh beside her and felt light without the heavy red wig of Caroline Anstretton.

A new beginning.

Another direction.

She hoped Thornton Lindsay's head would not be too sore. She hoped the man who rode with him was a friend. She tried not to notice the way his left hand threaded through the soft skin at his temple, massaging away pain. He was a duke of the realm, after all. His servants would see to his every need once he returned home. A bath, a good meal, and the prospect one day soon of a wife to warm his bed. A wife. Any wife? A girl of spotless name and rank and the truth of heart that he deserved after all his years of service.

She hated the stinging smart of tears in her eyes as she watched the coach doors shut without them on board and the driver call the horses on.

Now he would go too. For ever lost to her.

When the two men turned away she strained to see the last of them, as they disappeared into the thickening fog.

'The next coach leaves at one,' Tosh informed her as they backtracked with their one suitcase and entered a nearby tavern. The smell of food made her mouth water and the itchy wool of her nun's habit stretched full about her face. An easy disguise. She thought her brother suited his priestly robes and determined to tell him so as a group in one corner disbanded and made way for them to sit down.

God's people travelled well, she mused, when the tavern master refused payment for both bread and water.

Fingering the locket in her pocket, she smiled, the light of the fire catching the gold of the cross at her neck, reflecting beams across her brother's face. Tosh. Her saviour. Flesh-and-blood warmth, born from the sameness.

Tears blurred vision and she wiped her eyes against the generous cloth of her sleeve. Together they could hold the world at bay. And would. With a growing fervency she bent to a heartfelt prayer of thanks.

'You look rather changed from when I saw you last, Fox.'

Fox. The name he had used in the shady corners of the world where it paid to tell nobody your business.

'I cannot say, either, if the change is for the better or for the worse—I have always loved a damaged man, Your Grace.'

Following Adele Halstead into the salon, Thornton saw that she had lost none of her lithe beauty since he had last seen her, though her hair, once black, was now lightly silvered.

'I also have been told that it is you I have to thank for chasing off some intruders from my house. My servants were full of your bravery, though it seems they may have got the better of the exchange.'

'I am not the man that I used to be.' He tried to keep the irony light.

'Oh, I very much doubt that. Rumour has it that you are in London to discourage the advances of a...lover, and a woman of some notoriety, I am told.' She laughed. 'All of London is agog with the details of your meeting.'

Ignoring the banter, Thornton pulled the letter François had given him from his pocket and handed it over.

'This came into my hands two days ago and I recognised it as your writing.'

Puzzlement showed in Adele's face and then comprehension as she read the note. 'Lillyanna de Gennes?'

'Why did she not take heed of your warning?'

'I asked myself the same question at the time. As for my cousin, I would have thought her to have had a greater sense of self-preservation.'

'Yet you did not warn me.'

'You would never have believed me—though I had heard that there might be a problem, I did not know the details, and superstition in the field in the heat of the moment can be interpreted as a weakness. You could be a heartless bastard when anyone made a mistake, Thorn, and you had the ear of Wellington. I am surprised that Lilly did not confide my uneasiness to you.'

He broke into her diatribe. 'Enough. I am not here for excuses.'

'What are you here for, then?'

He held up the note. 'Was it you who set the trap?'

She shook her head and bitter anger burned in the back of Thornton's throat, the scars on his left cheek throbbing with the memory of everything, trust cast away in a barrage of cannon fire.

His life.

Her life.

The lives of fifteen of his soldiers.

Treason and loyalty, two sides of the same coin. France and England. War and peace. And a betrayal that was unexpected.

'I think you are lying.'

'Do you?' A calculated question. 'You always were so...honourable; if truth be known, it is a fault in the end, for no one else can quite live up to the standards you expect of them, not even Lilly. Besides, she had lost her own parents in the war to the British at the Battle of Maida and sometimes old loyalties rise up to stamp out new ones.'

A searing jolt of anger made his world blur, though he was careful not to let her see his fury. 'Lillyanna did not know about the French cannons stationed on the hill above the town.'

'You are certain of that?' The slur was distinct, though her laughter that held softer pity confused him. 'Perhaps Lilly did not warn you because then you would have known she was playing both sides off against the other.'

'As you were?'

'I am married to an English earl, Your Grace. Solid aristocracy and the wealth of generations. Why should I do anything to threaten that? Besides, I only ever dabbled in the game of espionage, and after this incident I returned to England cured of any need to pursue a career in it.' Pouring herself another cup of tea, she changed the subject altogether. 'Word has it that this beautiful widow, who swears you were once her lover, is from Paris? And a twin? I should have liked to have met her.'

He felt the slow turn of a familiar distrust as her interest and instinct took over. 'They left London two days ago on the Edinburgh coach and were hoping to spend some time with relatives. I doubt if I will ever see them again.'

'You know a lot about their movements?'

'That's my vocation. To find out as much about people as I possibly can.'

The silence between them lengthened and it was Adele who broke first.

'Well, then, let me test you. Did you happen to see the faces of the intruders the other night?'

'No. I was hit from behind as I entered your chamber. What was taken?'

'A purse of gold, some pearls and a fob watch.'

'Then you were lucky it was not more, for I counted at least three men in the shadows.'

For a moment Thornton saw uncertainty taint the arrogance in Adele's eyes.

'Did your husband return with you from Kent?'

'Yes. But he is ill in bed. A stomach upset from something he has eaten, I am told.'

'When he is better, I would like to talk to him.'

'I think it would be far better for us to just part company for good. My husband would not wish to be harried by the less salutary times in my life.'

'Because he has no idea that his wife was such a traitor?'

In reply she picked up a small bell from the table beside her and a footman came hurrying in.

'Yes, madame?'

'Could you show the Duke of Penborne out, please? He was just leaving.'

Thornton drew himself up from the chair that he sat in. 'Always a pleasure to speak with you, Lady Adele, and please do give my regards to your family.' He almost laughed at the cold hard line of her mouth as he found his cane and left.

In the carriage Thornton mulled over the conversation. Was she lying about the locket to protect her husband or herself? He had seen duplicity in the quick beat at her throat and the beaded sweat on her forehead when he had mentioned Wroxham and Adele Halstead did not want anyone to know the details of what had been taken in the robbery? Why should that be?

Clues that led nowhere. Ties that bound people without conceivable bonds. A note that gave a warning completely ignored. A locket stolen and then re-stolen. A war, whose tentacles reached into the present with echoes of betrayal. Words beneath words and the aching reminder of loss.

His fingers tightened on the carved ebony handle of his cane as loneliness welled unbidden. He had no one. London with all of its people accentuated that truth as Cornwall never had.

All he wanted to do was to go home.

But first he would interrogate the driver and the inn servants and try to match up Caroline and Thomas Anstretton with any new form of disguise they might have donned.

Chapter Six

August 1817

Readjusting the mask on her face, Caroline turned back to the ballroom, her silk dress catching the light of candles, the material shimmering gold.

Excitement coursed through her. It had been all of sixteen months since she had left London with her heart on her sleeve and the fifty guineas safely in her reticule. And in those months her life had taken a different twist again, the girl she had been submerged into the woman she had become. Wiser. More careful. And meticulous in her dealings with the opposite sex.

Her fingers checked the bun she wore and she tucked in the errant blonde curls that had escaped their confines during a dance with an elderly relative of the Hilvertons.

After leaving London, she had imagined she would

never grace a ballroom again, never feel the promise of youth and exuberance, never mingle with the local gentry with even a modicum of propriety. But she had, and a good deal of that fortune was due to Gwenneth Hilverton, the daughter-in-law of the Earl of Hilverton and the wife of the heir to this house and land and fortune. She had met Gwenneth by chance at a soirée in Bristol and been offered the chance of a cottage in return for portraits of her children.

Smiling, she crossed the room to stand by Gwenneth's side, warm fingers curling around her own in welcome.

'You look beautiful tonight, Caroline. The dress fits you as well as I thought it would.'

'And you are certain that you have worn it before. It looks too…new.'

'I wore it once when I was as thin as you are but that was some time ago. Malcolm keeps telling me to stop eating so much, though goodness knows I have tried.'

The mention of Gwenneth's husband brought a cloud over the euphoria of the evening and Caroline looked around furtively to make certain that the young Lord Hilverton was nowhere near. She had endured many a clandestine pinch on the bottom since she had come to this place, but had refrained from complaint simply because of the hurt it would bring to Gwenneth.

Her disguise as the prim widow ensured most men were happy to keep their distance. The spectacles probably helped, as did the rather stiff countenance she had now perfected, but Malcolm Hilverton was the one man who seemed attracted to her austerity.

Sometimes she wondered what Gwenneth had seen in him to make her accept his proposal in the first place. Rich in her own right, she had not needed to place her hand in that of a man who would scorn her at every available opportunity and treat her as a woman with very little of importance to say.

Caroline shook her head. Tonight she would not let problems impinge on excitement. She would enjoy the evening behind the safety of her mask and before midnight she would make very sure that she slipped away home through the little path to the cottage on the other side of the glade.

And become the Widow Weatherby again. Respectable. Proper. Reputable. The woman who lived quietly with her brother, making a living from fashioning portraits for the very well-to-do.

An irreproachable paragon, the likeness of a husband framed on the dining-room wall, a young husband lost off the coast of Plymouth in a storm that had overturned his boat.

Sometimes, with the sea winds soft off the Bristol Estuary and Alexander in her arms, she could almost believe the fabrication herself. And yet it was in those moments that the memory of Thornton Lindsay was strongest.

That awful scene in his library.

Vain. Selfish. Stupid.

The pain of deceit in his amber eye as Tosh had struck him in the darkened Halstead room. Falling. Again. The scars on his face white against moonlight.

No. No. No.

Safety depended on anonymity. And distance. And she had sold her soul to make certain that her brother should stay safe.

Shaking her head, she put her mind to enjoying the last hours of the evening, pulling Gwenneth towards the supper room where the lines of hungry guests were finally abating, pleased that the mask she had constructed hid her countenance.

'I am not certain that I should eat quite yet, Caroline. We have guests from London here tonight, and Malcolm says I must make an effort to draw them into conversation, but they look rather…menacing, so I have managed to avoid them all thus far. Particularly the taller man…' She petered out, pointing to a group on the other side of the room.

Alarming. Dark haired. Formidable.

Caroline's breath congealed in her throat. Thornton Lindsay stood dressed all in black, the ruined side of his face wreathed in a half-mask and a beautiful woman draped provocatively across his arm.

If Gwenneth had not held her up, she might have fallen; indeed, even as it was, she tipped forward, a whirling lightness unbalancing reality, her pulse in her temples beating so loud she thought everyone must hear it, must know it, must see that here, right here in this room, ten yards away, was a man whom she had once known…intimately. Bought and sold in lust.

Fear enveloped her and then a curious calm as he looked up, his eyes exactly as she remembered them, caution threaded with intelligence.

She made herself smile, made herself stand straighter, made herself breathe as he approached them, a whisper of a frown on his forehead.

'Lady Hilverton.' He held out one gloved hand, and the sound of his voice filled the cold draughty corridors of Caroline's heart and the pit of her stomach where the butterflies collided against exposure.

Could he know her? Would he remember? She did not dare to risk looking up in case he watched her and was pleased when Malcolm Hilverton pushed in between them, his face ruddy and his eyes full of self-importance. 'It is a great honour to have you here, Your Grace. I hope we can persuade you to stay on for at least a few days. Perhaps you would like to come riding tomorrow and partake in a picnic lunch with us down by the rocks of Morte Bay.'

'Perhaps.' His reply was abrupt and Malcolm, covering the awkwardness of the moment, pulled Caroline forward, his hand tarrying on the crook of her elbow for longer than she would have preferred.

'I would like to introduce you to Mrs Weatherby. She

has lived on the estate for more than a year now with her brother and baby son.'

Alex!

His amber eyes the mirror image of his father's and his hair the exact same shade of midnight black.

No future.

No contact.

No place for a woman such as her amidst the *ton* and a family that could trace their ancestry back for generations.

And no place for a bastard heir, either…

Glancing up, she saw his eyes upon her, questioning and unsettled, the unevenness of skin beneath the bottom edge of mask familiar. Dangerous. Risky. His visage toughened by a life that had allowed him little ease and a reputation that always kept others at bay.

'I understand you are here visiting your property, Your Grace,' Malcolm spoke in the tone of one with the full confidence of the other and even when one dark eyebrow tweaked upwards he continued unabashed. 'I could offer my services to familiarise you with local knowledge…'

'I have someone to help in that.'

Thornton Lindsay did not mince words or soften the message and the young woman standing beside him wound his arms through her own and tilted her head proprietarily, the ivory sheen of her skin making her look as if she were barely old enough to even be up so late.

Suddenly Caroline felt as if she were one hundred and one, lumped in now with the older matrons. A woman who was over the hill at twenty-two, placed as she was outside the boundary of any true and lasting relationship by a past that would crucify her in any and every salon of repute.

Looking up, she caught the full flare of the Duke of Penborne's gaze on her, abstruse and probing, and the room began to tilt.

Could he see her through the mask? Did he know? Had he remembered?

She ground her teeth together in pure fright. Let them move on, let them pass; let them return to wherever they had materialised from tonight. Far away from here and from her. Far away from memory and regret and the aching true knowledge of want.

Want—to take his hand in her own and never let go. Want—to lie down on the thick rug in his town house and feel things that she never had before and never would again.

Again.

Alexander!

The consequences were even greater this time and she could not afford the risk of anything.

Malcolm, true to form, was making the most of the moment, and his ridiculous comments were consolidated with his next outburst.

'I had heard that you have a team of fine horses with

you, Duke. Word has it they are of Arabian stock you had especially brought over to England.'

In Lindsay's glance Caroline detected a glimmer of surprise, though he answered with a semblance of polite distance.

'If you would care to look them over, you would be welcome. We will be remaining at Millington for the rest of the week.'

Six more days? Caroline pulled her mask more snugly against her cheek and frowned as she saw the Duke watching her fingers in a way that worried her.

Horses and houses. Heirlooms passed from one generation to the next. She and Tosh had missed out on such traditions and now Alex was going to do the same. Guilt sliced through reason and she turned away, ignoring Gwenneth's surprised query as she strode towards the door, tears seeping down inside her mask.

She had to get home, away from the lights and music and the whirling pressure of what could have been.

She had to get away from the dangerous Duke of Penborne.

She gathered herself together out in the silence of the cottage garden, the unfairness of everything diminished somewhat under a sky of twinkling stars. A beautiful night, summer in the air and the strains of Mozart far off in the distance.

Opening the front door, she found Tosh reading a

book, Alexander slumbering across his lap, his cherubic cheeks reddened by a cough he had developed over the past few days. She had never felt so glad to see them both, her anchors against the world.

'You look...worried.' Tosh carefully disengaged the sleeping baby and stood.

'Thornton Lindsay was at the ball.'

'Lord. Did he know you?'

She shook her head. 'I hardly spoke and the mask...'

'How long is he here for?'

'I am not sure. He actually owns one of the neighbouring estates.'

'We can find somewhere else to go.'

Love engulfed her. And sadness. For the first time in a long while she felt they had the chance to make something of their lives. Yet here her brother was, prepared to just up and leave.

She shook her head as his fingers curled up into hers. So familiar. So known.

'He has appointed a new manager for the farm and shall be here only fleetingly. Gwenneth introduced me as Mrs Weatherby.'

'You had your mask on?'

'I did, and I am certain that you cannot see my eyes through the feathers?' She held it in front of her face and was pleased when he shook his head.

'Even I would be hard pressed to know that it was you.'

Instantly she relaxed and crossed back to the sofa to

perch beside Alexander. 'Then I think I am still safe.' Her fingers pushed back a strand of darkness and her son shifted in his sleep, the faint warmth of his breath tickling the top of Caroline's thumb. 'But to be certain I think we should both stay in tomorrow. Malcolm made mention of a riding expedition and a picnic at Morte Bay. And if Lindsay should see us together…'

'I'm due in Exeter for the next few days to help Johnathon Wells at a cattle sale. Perhaps you could come with me.'

She shook her head. 'No, there is a portrait I have to finish and Alexander is grizzly. Besides, the Duke looked more than enamoured with his beautiful travelling companion.'

Tosh looked up sharply and Caroline held out her hand to stop him saying anything. She could see in the perplexity of his glance a raft of questions and did not feel at this moment up to answering even one of them.

Carefully she bent to lift Alex in her arms, his warm body moulding into her own.

Alexander Thornton Weatherby. In the moments of joy after his birth she had chosen the name of his father to also be his. A reminder and a keepsake.

She had known she was pregnant within three weeks of leaving London, a tiredness sweeping over her every movement and an utter sadness that she hadn't lost until the moment she delivered her son. When she had held him in her arms and felt the first tug on her breast, the inexplicable vagaries of her world had been healed, and her transient nomadic life had come to an end.

She had argued with herself as to whether she should contact Thornton Lindsay with her news. But the letter she had received after their night together had dissuaded her completely, his offer telling her exactly just where his heart lay. He did not want her for a wife. He did not even offer her a residence. Nay, he wanted a temporary liaison, a provisional and interim union whilst he looked elsewhere for a life-long partner.

A wife.

But not her!

Far better then for all concerned just to leave everything as it was. A chance meeting that would not be repeated. The beginning of a new life that contained none of the what-ifs of the old one.

She dashed away the tears with the back of her hand and went to settle Alexander, her world suddenly on the edge of teetering into chaos and negating everything she had so carefully built around herself over the past months.

Well, she would not let it. She would make certain that he did not know her, and would keep her ear to the ground so that she should discover the movements of the Millington party well before they could inadvertently come across one another again.

As she sang a night-time song to her son, tears scalded down her cheeks and her heart was heavy.

Thornton Lindsay.

Here.

Not even half a mile from where she sat.

Seeing the same moon.

Breathing the same air.

She chastised herself soundly for her silliness and tucked the blankets firmly about her son.

Thornton stood against the window and looked out across the dark valleys of this part of England. Civilised, rolling, manicured. None of the wildness of Cornwall with its untamed beaches and windswept coves, where long breakers eroded sandstone into jagged ramparts.

He felt stymied and caught, and he wondered about the turning his life had taken. He seemed to have lost something…inexplicable. Lord, he was twenty-eight and his conscious and calculated decision to take a wife wasn't turning out in quite the way that it should.

He muttered beneath his breath as he remembered another night, in London, the fifty guineas small payment for the hours that had followed.

The Weatherby widow had in some way reminded him of Caroline Anstretton. Strong. Unusual. Something in the turn of her head and the upward line of her lips.

He wished he could have removed her mask and seen her eyes.

Lifting a full glass of brandy, he remembered other things. The shape of her nails and the crescent scar at the base of her thumb as she had held her mask in place. White honeyed hair slightly curly.

And a baby son!

His mind began calculating back the months and came up with an answer that had his blood boiling.

It had to be Caroline Anstetton and—she was a mother.

And in that one simple moment of clarity he was glad that she was not standing there before him with her deceit and her vanity and her cold-hearted calculation.

Because he wondered if he could have stopped himself from placing his fingers around her beautiful throat.

Chapter Seven

Caroline dressed carefully, the thick glasses she had brought from London jammed hard over her nose, and leaving her to wonder if she should contemplate removing them. Already they gave her the beginnings of a headache and the bun stretched against her nape was uncomfortably tight.

Still she needed bread and some meat; at this early hour of the morning she was almost certain she would go unnoticed.

Anna, a girl from the village, had come to watch Alex whilst Caroline ran her errands and she was glad not to have to take her fretting son anywhere. Thomas had left even before she awoke, on his way to the cattle sales in Exeter, and she knew he wouldn't be home until the day after tomorrow at the earliest. If she made a stew today it would keep, and whilst it cooked she would try to work on the portrait she was completing of Gwenneth's youngest child.

A busy life, she thought, as she wandered down the path towards Campton. And safe. She would not let anything happen to compromise it.

This morning the sky was blue and the sun warm, a beautiful day with the promise of a hotter afternoon in the air. Her second summer at Campton. Would there be a third and fourth? She hoped so with all her heart and imagined Alex growing up here.

A satisfying life. A life bound not by what they could get, but by what they could give.

So different from her own upbringing, the halls of the Château du Malmaison on the outskirts of Paris filled with priceless baubles, and Guy de Lerin prowling around every corner. Nay, she would not think of him on such a day, for his lingering shadow of doubt and guilt dulled everything.

Campton was bustling with people as the market settled down for the morning's trading. Caroline glanced around quickly, making certain that no tall dark-haired stranger lurked amongst the crowd, her heartbeat quietening when everything seemed as it always was, though as she passed by the high fence to the left of the Selman's shop someone blocked her path.

Thornton Lindsay.

He had been waiting for her!

She could see it in his eye, dark flints of certainty unveiling deception.

The trickling dread became a torrent and dizziness swept across her. When he touched her arm, the heat from his hand sent a shock wave down into the very depths of her stomach and then darkness swallowed her.

She came to on a bed in an alcove at the back of the shop, and her glasses were gone.

Staying perfectly still she listened to the voices of those about her to try to determine safety.

'She has always seemed such a strong girl. I can't think why she should swoon like this.' Kathleen Selman's voice was as puzzled as her husband's.

'Should we send for her brother?'

'No, he is in Exeter, but someone has gone for the midwife. She will know what it is that ails her.'

'Perhaps another child?' Kevin Selman questioned, refraining from further speculation as the shocked gasp of Mrs Selman quietened him.

A child. A widow? Caroline's indignation gathered. She had spent the past sixteen months living on the moral high ground and still they could say this of her.

Where was Thornton Lindsay? As she struggled to get some sense of him, the tingling in her neck told her that he was close.

Opening her eyes just a little, she stared straight into his furious face.

And in his hand he held her glasses.

A heavy stain of blood rose up her cheeks and tears pooled. She was ruined. Exposed.

Waiting for him to say her name, she was surprised when he did not. Rather he handed her back her spectacles and stood, rigid anger in every line of his body.

Ignoring the pleas from Mrs Selman to stay lying down, she replaced her spectacles. Shakily. Not looking at him.

One word and chaos would claim her.

The very thought of it had her caught like a moth in flame. Nowhere to go.

Kathleen Selman bundled forward with a cold flannel and pushed the wet rag against her forehead.

'This should make you feel better, though I'm not quite so certain you should be standing.'

Caroline was pleased for the cloth that shaded her. Anything to hide behind. Even for a moment.

'It's an odd thing for a young lady to come over quite so dizzy, I'd be a-thinking, though perhaps the broken nights with young Alex—'

'It was the ball. I must have eaten something.' It was rude to break in over the woman's concerns but she wanted no mention of her son.

'I will escort you home.'

His voice, and one that brooked no argument.

'Oh, you do not have to do that, Your Grace, for I am almost recovered…'

'Bring around my carriage.' Thornton Lindsay signalled to his servant by the door as he laid his hand under her elbow. She felt the pressure of his fingers biting into her skin, and, short of making a scene, she had no option but to accompany him.

If she could get him by himself and plead her case, perhaps he might simply disappear. Leave. Responsibility happily relinquished in the face of opposition.

When he spoke as the carriage moved off, however, she knew that nothing would be easy.

'I want to see my child.'

'Your child?'

'Our child,' he amended. His knuckles were white. 'Alexander Thornton Weatherby?'

She swallowed back both bile and fear.

'How did you know…?'

'My purse is a hefty one and any information has a price.'

'I am the Widow Weatherby here. Prim. Proper. Eminently moral. Did you also discover that?'

His lips twitched. 'What happened to your husband?'

'He died.'

'How?'

'He drowned.'

'Very convenient of him.'

She did not look around.

'I want to see Alexander.'

'Why?'

'Because he is my son.'

'No. Alex is the son of a man who drowned off the south coast.'

'Whose name was Thornton?' His fingers bit into her flesh. 'Come now, Caroline. Play it fair. Alexander was conceived on the night of the fifteenth of April 1816 and for the payment of fifty guineas. His mother was a well-known harlot who was remarkably unskilled in the ways of *amour*.' He smiled at her sharp intake of breath. 'He is mine.'

Fright claimed her and the insides of her stomach began to clench as her breath shallowed, the burning pain of want betraying her sense of honour. When his thumb came up against the outline of a hardening nipple, shocking against the sunlight slanting in through the window, she gasped.

'The driver….'

'Will not stop until I tell him to.'

Anger consumed her. 'You think I am that easy? You think that you can come back into my life after sixteen months and expect…expect…. Again? Just like that? Here? No. I will not do it.'

'Ahh, but I think that you will. Is this your cottage?' He banged his cane upon the roof. Twice. And the carriage halted.

Absolute panic replaced everything when she looked outside, her small house with its profusion of creeping roses achingly familiar. Completely unprotected.

'Yes.'

'And our son is inside?'

Terror kept her mute.

'I will be here for a week and before those seven days have passed I would hope you could see sense and give me the truth of at least your name. Do you understand me?'

When he opened the door and she climbed down he did not wait for her answer, but tipped his hat and moved on, the hollow sound of her heartbeat muting the heavy hooves of the horses.

And then she ran. Into the cottage, past Anna busy in the kitchen and into the room where her son still slumbered, the small whiffs of his breath immeasurably reassuring.

'Alex.' If she lost him, she would die. Her son. His eyes opened suddenly, amber dark and beautiful.

'Mine.' The word was whispered beneath her breath, across her fear, over the beat of her heart and between the grasp of her shaking hands as she held him close.

He tried to wriggle from her grip.

'I love you, Alexander. You will always be mine.'

When he snuggled in she knew the exact moment that he fell fast asleep.

From the carriage, Thornton watched Caroline run from him, again, watched the sensuous tilt of her hips and the swish of her homespun gown. And his fingers tightened against his thigh as he stopped himself from following her.

She was furious, but he had no choice. A gentle reason and a well-hewn logic would have been preferable, but he could see the fear in her eyes over outright distrust. Better to seek out a solution when she had calmed down and then gain the access he wanted to his son.

Lord. His son? Were women always destined to deceive him? Adele Halstead's accusations about Lilly's betrayal that he could not quite dismiss, and now the Weatherby widow with her ridiculous denials of his fatherhood.

He could leave. He could return to Penleven right this moment. Keep driving and never look back.

But then what? A child would grow in the world without a father, a child with his name and his blood. A child that he had never seen or touched or known.

He slapped his hands hard against the door of the carriage and tried to think.

Caroline met him again the next day at a luncheon Gwenneth had arranged in the beautiful gardens at Hilverton. Tosh was still away in Exeter and Alexander had been carefully left at home.

This time she was prepared. Glad to see him even, her ire so raised as to almost welcome another encounter with the Duke of Penborne, though today in the company of these people he looked anything but comfortable, the collar of his jacket pulled well up over his jaw.

Distance, wealth and power enveloped him and the

arresting menace of his scarred face was shamefully fascinating.

Fawning, simpering, flirting women stood nearby: the Raymond sisters, the Furnesses. Even Gwenneth seemed swayed. Ice coated Caroline's veins and she plastered civility tightly across her demeanour. Sixteen months ago she was certain Thornton Lindsay would have never attended such an occasion and she wondered just what had changed to make him come.

'Your Grace.'

When he tipped his head and watched her there was a stinging tension in the hard line of his jaw and in his one uncovered eye she could see a vigilant, guarded anger.

'I trust you are feeling better today, Mrs Weatherby.'

At least he had remembered her name.

'Much, thank you, Your Grace.' She accepted a glass of punch and tried to look as nonchalant as she was able.

'I hear your brother is in Exeter.'

'He is. Yes, Your Grace, but when he is away I always have a local girl who sleeps over.' She needed to make it plain that she was hardly alone.

'Anna?' The surprised question in Gwenneth's voice grated as she joined in the conversation. 'I thought you said you enjoyed your own—' She stopped as the true message of the lie hit her and Caroline had to give her full marks for the way she dredged up another topic and ran with that one. 'How is the portrait of

Megan coming along? Why, I was saying to Malcolm just the other day how much I adore the one you did of young Jack.'

'You are an artist?'

For the first time since meeting him Caroline heard surprise in the Duke of Penborne's voice.

'I dabble with a paintbrush and charcoal to help pay the rent. Gwenneth is kind in her patronage.'

'She has made portraits of both my sons and of my mother-in-law. They hang in the main hall if you are interested in seeing them, Your Grace.' Gwenneth's eyes positively shone with support and even as Thornton began to speak Caroline knew exactly what he was about to propose.

'Would you consider taking on a commission from me? I would pay well.'

There was a titter of voices all around as the others overheard his suggestion. Envy combined with a good deal of shock. Today in the sunlight the markings on the left side of his face were well evident, his cheekbone dented in by a mass of lesions.

If the painting he spoke of was to be a portrait of him, she knew that he would never hang it in any one of his houses. No, it was time he sought. Long unadulterated spaces of it! Her heart raced because she knew that if she refused him outright there would be questions.

Already she could see a frown on Gwenneth's brow at her tardiness.

'Of course, I shall be delighted to.' She tried to insert some enthusiasm into the acceptance.

'Would tomorrow suit, then? I could send over my carriage to fetch you after lunch.'

With no other recourse left she nodded her thanks, turning towards the table where an expansive array of food was set and helping herself to a plate. With her mouth full at least she would be excused from any conversation.

She was the Widow Weatherby. Pious. Circumspect. Grateful. And any hint of something else would raise a suspicion she could ill afford.

Tucking her blonde hair up under an ugly cap, she admonished herself for even thinking that she could play the Duke of Penborne at his own game. He had been a soldier and a spy. The kind that hung like a ghost in the trouble spots of the world, coaxing intelligence from the population with whom he mixed. He wanted answers from her, and an explanation of the different circumstances under which she now lived. The virtuous widow was a long way, after all, from the woman he had once known briefly but intimately in London, and a longer way still from the thief he had disturbed in the night-dark rooms of the Wroxhams' town house.

Questions. She could see in his eyes that which had been reflected in countless acquaintances across the years.

Who are you?

I am a murderer. I am a liar. I am a survivor. The

smaller whisper from inside her was stark. Unremittingly honest. Desperately powerful.

Subduing her horror, she turned to one of the Furness girls standing nearby and made herself contribute to a conversation about the new season's fashion, even as a trickle of sweat made its way down between the heat of her breasts.

Thornton watched Caroline as she chatted with another young woman. Today she looked tired, the violet rings beneath her eyes giving her a bruised and fragile countenance.

He would not let guilt rise. After all, she had hidden their child away from him and, as yet, refused to acknowledge his fatherhood.

The Widow Weatherby had changed her name and her profession, and ended up here in the Bristol estuaries, painting portraits for the aristocracy.

He had to smile—Caroline Anstretton never ceased to confound him.

Yet where was it they went from here? He knew almost nothing about her and the thought worried him.

If he could get her alone tomorrow even for a few hours under the guise of a portrait sitting, perhaps he could find out who she was, where she was from, who her family were and what it was she believed in.

He hated the necessity of being here and of accepting an invitation to a party of women with little else on their minds save the snaring of a rich husband. But he was caught by Caroline's indifference and by time, which allowed him only a few days in this corner of England. Lord, if he could have walked away this minute with her on his arm he would have, but she was doing her level best to stay well out of his proximity. Even so, he felt her eyes upon him, though when he turned she made much of appearing distracted by those closest to her.

His left eye throbbed with the beginnings of a tic that came when he was tired. All he wanted was to be alone with Caroline. All he wanted was to feel again the warmth of her skin against his own and the heady smell of roses.

A child.

His child.

Their child.

Together.

As the sun slanted down on to corn-blonde curls he felt his world turn into place.

Simple.

Easy.

He closed his eyes momentarily against the very ache of it and tried to appear interested in the lesson on local history that the well-meaning pastor of the village was regaling him with.

And when he looked around again five moments later, she was gone.

Chapter Eight

'Is there a particular angle or feeling you would wish me to capture?'

'I think we both know that you did not come here to draw my portrait, Mrs Weatherby.'

Caroline's heart sank. She had been at Millington for less than two minutes and already the tone of this meeting was disintegrating.

Squaring her shoulders, she put down her painting satchel and took in breath. 'I hope you do not believe that I have come to…' *Bed you, sleep with you, do what we did in London.*

She could not quite say it and so changed tack. 'I am more than certain that you would not insist on intimacy if a woman was saying no. Which I most definitely am, Your Grace. Saying no. To anything.'

'I see.' The light in his amber eyes was not as menacing as she might have imagined after such a confession. Indeed, he looked almost amused.

'Why am I here, then?' Suddenly she had had enough, this exhausting charade sweeping away politeness.

He took a moment before he answered, but the gist of his message was anything but hesitant. 'I want to know who you are. I want to know something, anything, about the mother of my only child. And I want to see him. I want to see Alexander.'

'I do not think that would be such a good idea.'

'Do you not?' Absolute stillness followed the question.

'No. I think it would be better if you simply believed my story and left.'

'Which story? None of the versions you have regaled me with so far quite add up.'

'I needed money in London. You offered it.'

'From all accounts there were many others in society who were offering a lot more.'

'I did not want marriage.'

'Ahh.' He walked right up to her, his face not six inches from her own. 'And therein lies my dilemma, Miss Anstretton. A beautiful woman who, for all intents and purposes, has no past?'

Fear kept Caroline silent. What could he find out after all? It had been a few years since they left Paris by way of many other cities and countries. Still, there was something about the Duke of Penborne that made her believe he could uncover any secret, and with Alexander between them she knew she would need to be wary. And conciliatory.

'You afford me a more mysterious and enigmatic background than I in truth do have, Your Grace. I am simply a woman who has encountered some hardships in life and is trying to keep her head above the murky water of debt. The silly vacuous girl you encountered all those months ago has long since gone and, should I have been faced with the same problems now as I was then, I would have certainly taken a different course in solving them.'

'I see. And you are what…twenty-two now?'

'Next birthday I shall be twenty-three.' She was cautious in her reply.

Anger shifted across his face. Bitter and distant, the whiteness of his scarred cheek opaque against the light in this room. Her heartbeat raced as the quicksilver pangs of desire rolled in her stomach. Upwards.

Always.

If she could just reach out and touch him. To see. To see if what had happened before could happen again.

But she couldn't. Because if he stepped back, what was left of her heart would surely break.

'I departed from London because I knew that if Thomas had met you he would have challenged you to a duel and he has not half the skill at weaponry that you are rumoured to have.'

'You think I would have killed him?'

She shrugged her shoulders and tried to lower her

voice. 'I think that you might have hurt him in the dead of some night when you had both had one too many brandies. And I could not take the chance.'

'So you ran?'

'Yes.'

'Why here?'

'We closed our eyes and placed a finger on the map.'

He smiled, dangerously, the gold in his eyes brittle sharp.

'How much would you charge for a portrait of yourself, completed here, at Millington, for as many afternoons as it took?'

'A picture of me? I do not know why you should want—'

He didn't let her finish. 'I would also like a portrait of my son. That you may fashion at your own leisure.'

'I am not certain—'

'The portrait, or meeting him in person, Caroline. Your choice.' His voice was hard, the softness of compromise completely gone, and all the fight left her body.

'As you wish.'

'I have had a table brought in, and a mirror.' His glance flicked to the satchel she held that contained all her equipment. The alcove he led her to was filled with light, two chairs standing at right angles to each other and an empty easel between them.

He would stay and watch? The thought unnerved her but she could not afford to lose the commission.

With care she sorted out her paints and charcoal, laying a cloth down so as to keep her canvas clean.

Blank. White. The gesso on the frame waiting for colour and shape. Her shape. She had not painted her likeness before and hesitated as her eyes met his in the mirror.

'How would you like me to stand?'

'Straight on.' His hand rested beneath her elbow and when he did not let her go she took in a breath and held it.

Kiss me, she longed to ask. Take me again. Here in the light of your house and without payment. The latent ache in her belly strengthened as she felt her nipples pucker, hard against his nearness.

But she could not say it, could not take again in lust what she had done so earlier in greed. Twenty-two and a mother. The responsibilities in life had her pulling away as she took up the charcoal and drew the first lines of her face, hoping that he did not notice the way her hand shook.

Thornton watched her, the smallness of her fingers bruised with smudges of old paint and her nails as short as he had seen on a woman.

Like her hair.

It was tucked into a bun but stray tendrils were escaping. And she still wore her gold bracelet, the fake glass emeralds dulled by age.

'If I looked up the Anstretton family lineage, where should I find your names?'

'Nowhere.'

Her glance met his head on.

'Because Anstretton is as false as Weatherby?'

'Yes.' She did not elaborate.

'Does the reason for such secrecy lie in the inscription on your bracelet, by any chance?'

Her face paled so alarmingly he thought she might faint. An answer.

Paris 1807—TStC.

He would work on the clues later and see in which direction they would take him.

'I should be pleased if within the time you take to complete this portrait you could entrust me with the truth of at least your name.'

When she nodded, the bleakness of her expression told him that she acquiesced only because he had demanded it and told him also that she had absolutely no intention at all of letting him close.

'You may be interested to know that Adele Halstead claimed a string of pearls, a fob watch and a purse of gold were the only things taken from her house the night you stole the locket.'

'You saw her?' Fear gave her query a breathless huskiness.

'In London, a few days after I found you in her rooms. I thought it prudent not to mention the fact of your visit, though I did wonder as to why she might have lied about the items taken.' He watched her blue eyes darken. 'If you would trust me, I may be able to help you—'

She stopped him by breaking over his offer with a breathless laugh.

'There is nothing you could help me with, Your Grace.'

Thornton recognised in her the same stubbornness he often saw in himself and he smiled.

'Were your parents also skilled as thespians?'

'You have been too long the spy, Your Grace,' she said sweetly with a touch of humour.

'And you have been too long on the run, Mrs... Weatherby.' Admiration drove a wedge of respect into his answer as he deliberately left a pause before her name. ''Tis in my mind that Adele Halstead kept the trinket for a reason, hidden in a drawer of her room.'

The bottom of her chin began to shake and she held her hand up against it. In the folds of her fingers Thorn could see the too-quick beat of the pulse at her neck. But he could also see the woman he had known in London, breathtakingly beautiful and frightened, and it was this vulnerability more than anything that made him stop.

'I will expect you tomorrow, at exactly the same time and we will continue our discussion.'

When he bowed and left, Caroline stood very still. In this sun-bleached room above the stairs with the light streaming in, tears drenched her eyes.

Worthiness. Intelligence. Acumen.

Replacing one canvas with another, she began to

draw. From memory. The lines of his face bold against the pureness of light. Exposing everything in the way that she saw it.

Beautiful.

Honourable.

Tarnished by the glory of war rather than by the agony of it. Scars that lay in bravery and valour and in the unflinching courage of conviction.

She had heard the rumours.

And seen the man.

Complex. Layered. Tortured.

If you trust me, I may be able to help you.

If their crime had not been so heinous, she almost believed that he could have. But no one could change what had happened. Even him.

An hour later the first lines of the portrait were complete and, tucking Thornton Lindsay's likeness beneath her own, she tidied her working space and left the house without once looking back.

She lay in bed that night and hated the hot tears that scalded down her cheeks, running with all the pent-up fury of her life so far.

One chance.

This chance.

If he left, she would not see him again. Ever.

The memory of the afternoon was close in the careful rendition of her face, fire in her eyes watching. Him.

Even in her rough charcoal sketch she had drawn the lines of a woman who wanted.

Would he see it too? She was certain that he must.

But why would he want this picture of her?

Why would he pay for a portrait that could mean nothing to him? That he could never hang?

A small flurry of hope fluttered before she pressed it back.

Today had been surprising.

Instead of argument there had been a kind of exultant truce, a reckless familiarity, a *détente* that was as heady as the slow burning want in her stomach. He had barely touched her; indeed, he had stood back as she had fashioned the first lines of the portrait, silent in his consideration of her drawing. And yet every pore of her body had been cognisant of the fact that their breath mingled and the warmth of his skin touched the coldness of her own.

She remembered her mother's tales about the court of Josephine de Beauharnais in the heady time before General Bonaparte had dispensed with her services. The days when her mother had laughed and danced, sheltered by Josephine's friendship at the Château du Malmaison.

'The good Lord in his wisdom provides one soulmate for each man and woman, Caroline,' her mother had told her just before she had died, the light and airy flightiness that had been so much a part of her personality dimmed by the nearness of an impending eternity. 'Josephine found hers in Napoleon, a man whom the whole world feared. Be wary in your search, my daughter, and do not squander such a chance as carelessly as I did.'

The shadows in the room grew, pulling Caroline backwards to a corridor overlooking the gardens, the shadow of plane trees long against the true green sweep of lawn and the first crocuses pushing their way up through the frozen earth.

Cold hands across her breast as she was arched downwards to the floor, Aubusson carpet and parquet.

And Thomas, furious, the bust of marble in his hand heavy and the look on Guy de Lerin's face puzzled.

Just another tryst with a young girl who would one day be more willing. An easy conquest. A meaningless dalliance to lighten the load of dark winter days and inclement weather.

Too late he had understood the extent of Caroline's resistance and the special bonding of twins.

They had slid him into the cupboard above the small landing on the second floor, his hat covering the rising bruises, his coat soaking up the blood from his nose, his face a deathly white. Broken. Badly. It would not matter. Hell had no need for beauty and his outer appearance mirrored his inner soul.

They had barely looked backwards after they fled, making their way south across the countryside where they had come across Adele Halstead on the outskirts of Orthez. Lord, she probably had their mother's locket in her luggage even then, stolen in the last moments of Eloise's life after pretending such an interest in her dying days.

But why? Why should she do such a thing?

Caroline's heart began to race as she thought about what happened next and, skipping across the danger, she remembered running into the Pyrenees mountains of Spain, two young lads of fortune. The first of their disguises.

How many had there been since? Shaking her head, she refused to even contemplate such a question.

Hiding.

For ever.

A single tear fell against the back of her hand and she watched it slide down between the gully of her fingers, a trail of coldness against the warmth of skin. And the wedding ring that sat there seemed to mock her, call her a liar, remind her that she would never have the luxury of intimacy with anyone.

Imitation and falsity were the calling cards of those who had broken the cardinal rules of humanity. And murder sat at the very top of the list of the Ten Commandments.

Thou shalt not kill.

The face of Guy de Lerin seemed to gloat from a netherworld, a battered spectre demanding redress. Caroline wondered if the image would ever fade, the bright red blood on his forehead mingling with shocked and disbelieving leaf-green eyes.

* * *

The knock came much later.

Her eyes slid across to the cot of her sleeping son and she clenched the material of her skirts into her fingers, caught in an immobile frozen uncertainty.

'Mrs Weatherby. Are you in?'

Johnathon Wells. Tosh's friend.

Hurrying to the door, she unbolted the locks, apologising for her tardiness, and instantly alarmed by the worried look on his face.

Thomas? Where was he? She could feel the beat of her heart in her throat as an ache.

'Your brother did not meet me at the arranged place today, ma'am, and neither did he accompany me home. The last I saw him was in the evening of yesterday enjoying a tipple in the Dog and Cart Tavern on Dilworth Street.'

'My God.' The very worst had happened. The fear that she had been burdened with since running from the Château du Malmaison, realised. Clutching at the lintel on the side of the door, she tried to steady herself, tried to listen to just what it was that Johnathon Wells was saying to her, tried not to let the vision of Tosh with his neck sliced open consume her.

'He did not return home to the lodgings last night and his bag is still there with the landlady. I left it with a message to say I had returned to Campton and that you would be worried.'

'Thank you.' The words stuck in her throat, making her swallow as she tried in the midst of fear to find a way out.

'Could I call someone for you, Mrs Weatherby? You look ill.'

'No.' She made herself smile. 'I am certain there will be a reason.'

The furrow on his brow told her he didn't believe her, but manners had him bidding her a good day and turning down the path.

Inside again, Caroline re-bolted the door and took three deep breaths. Panic made her hands shake and she closed her mouth tight to stop the scream of hysteria that threatened.

Alexander was in the next room and Tosh needed someone who would not go to pieces. Someone who would think and plan and do. The de Lerin family had taken him. She was certain of it. They had discovered where they were and come for retribution.

The Dog and Cart Tavern on Dilworth Street. A starting point at least.

She could not go as herself, that much was clear, and she would need to take the handgun that Tosh kept in the bottom drawer of his desk. It was a duelling pistol finished in walnut and engraved with gold inlays, the richness of the scrolled barrel recalling the heady days of Paris.

She smiled to herself as she wrapped the firearm in

soft chamois. Her brother had taught her to shoot with it and she still remembered clearly the basic details of the loading mechanism. If anyone had hurt Tosh, she would have no compunction whatsoever about shooting them.

Thornton tethered his horse against the fence in front of the Weatherbys' small cottage. Caroline had not come in the carriage that afternoon to work on her portrait and he was concerned.

He could tell nobody was at home even before he knocked on the door, and was about to leave when a young woman came up the path behind him.

'Caroline Weatherby has gone, Your Grace,' she said shyly and blushed a bright red.

'Gone where?'

'To Exeter. Alexander, her son, is up at the big house with Lady Hilverton, Your Grace.'

'And her brother?'

'That's the strange part, sir. He didn't come home with Johnathon Wells and I think Mrs Weatherby was very worried about him.'

'How long is she expecting to be away?'

'A good few days, I'd be thinking. The bag she took was hardly small and she asked Lady Hilverton the directions for Dilworth Street before she left. Down by the river it is and not a place I'd have thought she would have favoured. But cheap, maybe. She did ask me to water her garden if it was dry, though, and that's why I'm here.'

Thornton looked around. A window at the back of the house remained unfastened.

A quick exit, he surmised, Alexander sequestered at Hilverton Hall and the maid despatched to watch over the house.

Bidding the girl good day, he untied his horse's reins from the palings at the front gate and swung upon the back of the animal.

Dilworth Street. My God. He had been to Exeter a number of times in his youth and knew the area even if Caroline did not. He tried to determine just how fast he could get there.

Chapter Nine

It was late, almost ten-thirty when Thorn arrived at the Dog and Cart Tavern, the last of the watering holes on this side of the street, and the sound of earnest drinking was spilling out into the night. Bidding his men to wait with the carriage on a road opposite the establishment, he pulled up his collar and stepped inside, his fingers curled around the handgun primed and ready in his pocket.

A number of people stood in a large group to his right, though as he tuned into their conversation he felt no threat at all.

Further away a series of harlots worked the room, their costumes garish in the brightened light and, on a plinth to one end, a group of men were drinking themselves stupid. Instantly his hackles rose.

One of the whores moved towards them with a large tray of ale and when a man fondled her ample breasts she swatted his hand away playfully, egging on rejoinders from those next to him.

Something about her seemed familiar and when she turned and her profile was silhouetted against the light, a growl of pure disbelief sounded in Thornton's throat.

Caroline Anstretton/Weatherby!

Her cheeks were whitened with an almost theatrical make up and she wore large silver hoops in both ears.

What the hell was she doing here, dressed like that?

No longer thin, the padding in her harlot's gown portrayed her as a buxom and easy girl, with the accent of the docks in her words to boot.

'Ye'd be wantin' a warm night in a cosy bed, I suppose, sir? How many of you could I favour?'

Laughter built as she pulled one man's head into the charms of her bosom, though when he reached out to touch what she offered she moved back. Quickly.

'It's payment I'd be wantin', sir, and me room's not far.'

The long tresses of her black wig stuck to the thick pan make-up on her face and her tongue circled red-rouged lips in a singularly sensual movement.

Thornton felt a thickening want and looked away.

Lord, what was she making him become? The same leer of sexuality on his face was reflected in those of the group as they looked her over.

An easy charmer. Already one man stood adjusting the line of his trousers as his hand reached into his pocket for coinage. 'What's a night worth, me darlin'?'

Dark blue eyes flashed uncertainly.

'The price of a drink first, if ye don't mind. I've a thirst for cognac.'

As she sat down the outline of a small pistol was just visible below her left-hand sleeve. So she had come prepared, but how well could she use the weapon? Thornton watched as she made much of topping up even quarter-empty glasses.

Information. That was what she was trying to gather. Information about her brother and his movements. He wondered why she had singled out this lot of patrons given there were several other groups that seemed more…lawless. Perhaps it was simply the position of the table, placed as it was on a higher level than the rest of the tavern and facing the door.

He was pleased she had not seen him, though as he turned away a gaudily dressed older woman laid her hand across his arm.

'Is there a girl who has taken your fancy, guv'na? We have rooms upstairs.'

An idea formed as he looked at his timepiece.

'The black-haired whore. How much?'

Desperation began to assail Caroline as the night wound down into the minutes after midnight.

She had recognised nobody. She had heard neither a thick French accent nor seen a face with the lines of the de Lerin family stamped upon it and no whisper of any information about Thomas had surfaced. The coinage she had slipped the older woman for the chance to work the room had also been wasted.

Even now as the tavern master began to wipe down the tables and sweep the floor, no last customers tarried, lingering either inside or out in an effort at communication.

What should she do?

Call the constabulary?

Tears washed her eyes and fear licked at the lining of her stomach.

Thomas.

Where are you?

Shutting her eyes, she tried to imagine him in these surroundings. She had heard of this particular gift of twins many a time, but had never felt it herself. Perhaps in such dire circumstances….

The tug at her shoulder had her up and off the seat in a second, though she relaxed as she saw it was the older woman in charge of the girls here.

'There is a gentleman who would like to speak with you upstairs.'

'Gentleman?'

She handed over two gold coins. 'We like to keep it clean here, you understand. No funny business.'

Disorientation assailed Caroline. Had she been recognised even in this disguise? Her head began to ache with the dilemma.

Was this merely a harmless sexual proposition or

was it the work of a well-thought-out plan, for, alone and sequestered in an upstairs salon, she would be vulnerable. Yet if it were the de Lerins and she did not take up the opportunity to meet with them, what might happen to her brother?

Would they kill him?

She was caught and the clock was ticking away a chance.

Carefully she stood, accepting the money from the woman.

'Could you tell me a little about what he looks like?'

'He's wealthy, dearie. What else does a girl in your position need to know?'

'I am not certain how safe…'

'We'll look after you, don't worry. Any problems and you just need scream, Harry here can see to anyone.' A large man materialised out of the darkness behind her, a velvet cloak draped around his shoulders and a cap of sorts perched on his balding head. Indeed he did look as if he might deal with anybody and for the first time that evening Caroline relaxed. If she saw it was one of the de Lerin men, she would scream before he even had the time to cross the floor towards her and when Harry had done his worst she could then grill him with her own questions.

And if it were a stranger just there to gather a whore for the evening, she would turn and leave straight away. Her gun was in her sleeve, after all, and she knew how to use it.

'Very well.' Pulling down her wig more firmly, she followed the woman upstairs and took a deep breath before she stepped into the room.

It was darker than she had expected inside, a fire glowing dull against the far wall and not a single lantern lit. Before her eyes could even acclimatise to the dimness, a hand reached out from behind, cutting the circulation from her throat and bringing her body full against his, the gun she held clattering to the floor. Useless.

'Ooooolp,' she tried to shout as she stamped down upon the instep of her assailant's boot, and was rewarded with a harsh whisper against her cheek.

'I would strongly advise ye to keep very quiet.'

Her heart almost stopped in fright. Would he hurt her? Or worse?

Cursing, she tried her hardest to draw breath. His fingers smelt of soap, as if in the moment before she had come into the room he had washed his hands.

At least he was clean!

Such a ridiculous thought had her shaking her head even as his other fingers made free with her body, trailing over her breasts and pulling at the fragile lace that covered her cleavage.

Within a second his hand lay inside, thumb effortlessly stroking her nipple into hardness. Horrified, she stiffened, striking out with her hands, trying to loosen his hold as he spoke again.

'Gold coins and the middle of the night. How seriously can I take a refusal, lassie, dressed as ye are.'

Scottish. He was Scottish. With renewed fervour she banged her elbow against the wall behind, the sound surprisingly loud. Surely Harry would come. Surely someone must hear.

Five seconds went by and then ten. No knock at the door, no footsteps down the corridor. Nothing but the aching silence of the house closing around her with a growing and terrible certainty.

She should never have come here, should not have risked herself as carelessly as she had, the plan formulated on the way to Exeter ridiculous now in its clumsy execution.

He would rape her and she would be truly ruined.

For ever.

Struggling, she tried to force his hand from her mouth. Perhaps if she reasoned with him, offered him money….

Unexpectedly his tongue caressed the skin at her neck, a single trail of feeling.

Warm.

Soft.

A tangible echo in her mind of another night!

She stilled, waiting, disorientated by familiarity as his palm pushed inwards against her stomach. Lord. When his fingers trailed down further her eyes widened.

She really was a whore. Like her mother.

One sob and she was free, panting in her deliverance, not a single thought running through her mind save the despair of what she had become. Easy. Loose. Wanton.

'St...st...stay away. This is not right.' She could not find it in herself to even scream.

His shadow loomed in the dimness, and an expletive filled the room as he turned her back easily against him, wig entwined in a tangled web of blackness.

'Enough, Caroline.' The desultory tone bereft of accent surprised her and in that second she saw just exactly who her assailant was.

Thornton Lindsay, deep shadows bruising his one good eye.

'You.' Her palm slapped hard against the uneven skin on his left cheek and in reply he came in closer.

'Aye, and 'tis my view, Mrs Weatherby, that any woman who risks her life, as you just have, deserves at least a fright.'

Shame kept her still.

He had seen. He had known. Her pretended piety was a damning contradiction to the truth of her nature.

Fury roiled through her at the thought, though as she kicked out long fingers closed across her knee, warning her to stop.

She hated him. She did. She hated the way he could, with merely a single touch, make her body dissolve into a desperate sensual longing.

Again.

Like before.

Sweat beaded her forehead and dampened the place between her breasts as his hand on her knee travelled higher, teasing, provoking, the tantalising feel of pressure sending shivers into her very core.

'You planned all this,' she threw at him, hating the tears that ran down her face as delayed fear had her shaking, the torn chemise hiding little against his gaze when the fire caught and momentarily blazed bright.

'Hardly, madam. If I had not been here—' His voice was hoarse, but she did not let him finish.

'I would now be in my room along the road.'

'With one of the drunken patrons who was eyeing up your movements and more than interested in your bounteous charms.' He plucked out the layers of padding and for the first time she felt the hard heat of him against her skin; the air, already charged between them, became red hot.

'I prefer slimmer women, with long lithe legs, and a bust that needs no enhancing.' Drawing out the contraption that she had tied to her chest, he hurled it into the corner with the other accoutrements. 'A harlot. And paid for. Ahhh, Caroline, but it seems we have been in this place before.' His hips pushed in against hers, testing the waters, seeking what it was between them, sensuality vibrating with an ache. And when his fingers tipped her face up to his own, forcing her to look at him, she simply went to pieces.

Gold carnality shone forth in his eye. Lust and want completely unhidden in a man who normally guarded every nuance of his expression.

'I want you.' His whisper held more than a hint of desperation, words melting into feeling as he lifted her skirt, the night air cold against her thin petticoat. Ripping it off her with one twist, the lawn pooled at her ankles.

Surrender.

Anger.

The heady joy of coupling.

No one emotion, no single explanation.

Only feeling.

Only him.

His fingers opened the throbbing thickness between her legs and, lifting her up on to the hilt of his sex, he plunged in without hesitation.

Tight. Wet. Yielding. Filling her with heat.

Punching into the question of what lay between them with an uncompromising certainty. Taking her. Completely. No arguments. Now.

She cried out. Not in pain. And he laughed. The sweat on his brow as beaded as that on her own, the scent of their bodies slick, moistened and pungent.

Heaven.

She was there.

Again.

Her toes curled in loose leather shoes and her breath

broke as his did, waves of wonder rolling across them, and the rough wall behind.

Release. Relief. Deliverance.

Even her lungs forgot how to breathe as she arched backwards, his groans in rhythm with her own.

Another noise, loud and urgent, and furious shouting as the heavy banging at the door finally registered.

Thornton thrust her away, off him, even as she fought to stay, a veil of languid unconcern between her and the world. Still.

With quick hands he flipped her skirt down and grabbed his jacket from a nearby chair to cover her shoulders.

And then the door was agape. Flung open. Malcolm Hilverton stumbling inwards, Gwenneth and Tosh at his back.

Tosh?

Silence. Punctuated only by her friend's plaintive and sobbing cry.

'Oh, my God, Caroline. What have you done?' The furrow on her brow denoted horror and grief. 'I hope that you realise you are now completely and utterly ruined.'

Ruined!

Thornton pushed Caroline behind him and stepped forward. To explain. What?

With her black wig hanging to one side, red lip paint smeared across her cheek and her clothing torn, she did indeed look…ruined.

By him.

Utterly.

'It is not as you might think—' he began before his explanation was cut short, Caroline's lost brother hurling himself from the door against him and pushing him off balance. Both he and the boy crashed to the floor and Thornton felt the sharp cut of broken glass pierce his arm.

Lifting away, he turned to fend off Malcolm Hilverton, who had come to aid Thomas Anstretton, his rotund paunchiness easily dealt with. A single right-hander to the ears and he was quiet, though in the interim Anstretton had collected himself and fronted another attack.

The boy was certainly brawnier than he had been in London, the country air making short work of a card player's softness, and it was several moments before he felt like he was getting the better of the situation, Caroline's screams to not hurt her brother grinding at his sense of honour.

Thorn's arm streamed with blood and she was barely taking the time to notice. Why, even as her brother came in to attack him again she had the thick end of a broom pushed down hard, and his hands opened under reflex as he staggered against the remaining intact chair in the room, regrouping.

Her twin's nose bled profusely as the boy slid down the wall, red staining both the floor and Caroline's skirts as she bent over him, cuddling close. With her wig discarded, the shade of their hair was exactly the same in this light.

Whispering.

Shaking.

No one else existed in that room. Certainly he did not, the steady drip of blood from his fingers unnoticed. Lifting his elbow, he jammed it into the bony ridge of his right hip to stop the flow and tried to make sense of tonight.

Love.

Hate.

Loss.

Henry had come to stand at the door, awaiting instruction.

'I think it would be better if you left.' Gwenneth Hilverton's voice from the side of the room where she crouched over her groggy husband.

Caroline said nothing.

The sound of running feet outside. The local constabulary, he supposed, and cursed roundly.

If he were found here, scandal would ensue, his name grand enough for the cheap broadsheets to be more than interested in a story. And by association Caroline would also be tarnished. Nationally.

'There is an exit out the back, Your Grace.' Henry gestured to a door to one end of the passageway, and a dizzy tiredness forced Thornton to follow.

Within a moment they were in the side street and then he was ensconced in his coach, thick woollen blankets laid against a gathering coldness.

'Stay awake, sir.' The worried voice of Henry pierced a receding reality as the conveyance turned into the inn, the red light of the carriage lamp dancing strangely in a gathering wind.

Chapter Ten

'You cannot stay at Hilverton.' Gwenneth wept over the words quietly. 'Malcolm is not a person who could ever condone such…looseness and these are his lands.'

'Of course.' Caroline handed a handkerchief into Gwenneth's shaking fingers and tried to console her.

'I told him I would refuse to acknowledge the gravity of what happened in Exeter should he feel the need to repeat it to…anyone at all, and he threw a passage from the Psalms at me… "Who shall ascend into the hill of our Lord? He that hath clean hands and a pure heart."' Watery eyes raised up to her own. 'What was I to say to that, I ask you. He is a devout man…' She began sobbing again, this time without even an attempt at quietness. 'He said that he would honour my wants so long as you left. By the end of this week.'

Caroline's spirits fell. Three days. And the weather

unseasonably wet and cold! She could not even imagine where to begin, where to go and this time with a child in tow.

'Malcolm told me to say that your brother still has a place here if he should want it; after all, it is not his fault that you…that you…'

The accusation of immorality sat in her eyes, and in the quivering distaste upon her lips. 'Surely you must know that Thornton Lindsay would never marry you. He is a duke, for goodness' sake, and you met him for the first time less than a week ago?' Her voice strengthened considerably. 'For the life of me, I cannot comprehend the reasoning that should make you behave in such a manner and so…out of character, Caroline.'

'I am certain you cannot.'

Angry grey eyes lifted to her own before she pocketed the handkerchief and stood. 'This will be goodbye, I am afraid, as I shan't be requiring the finished portrait of my Megan under the circumstances. I would, however, like to give you this. It is saved from my own pin money, you understand, and money that my husband has no notion of. I want you to use it for Alexander. For his education.'

A heavy purse clunked down on the table before them.

Friendship. It was never black and white, Caroline mused, and the greys sometimes had the propensity to break your heart.

She swallowed before she spoke.

'I will never forget you.'

For the first time a small smile blossomed around tightened and disapproving lips. 'And I am certain that I could say exactly the same.'

When the door closed Thomas came forward from the side room where he had watched the conversation, undetected.

'She is a fine woman.'

'And a generous one.' Her fingers felt the number of coins in the leather.

'Pity you cannot tell her the truth, then.'

'Which is?'

'That you love Thornton Lindsay, the Duke of Penborne. That you have loved him since your first tryst in London when he fathered your only child.'

'A monogamous whore, then. But a whore none the less. Did you not hear her recited passage from the Bible?'

'I tried not to.'

For the first time in days Caroline actually laughed; the sadness she had been etched with since Lindsay had deserted her in Exeter relegated for a moment to some place distant.

Where had he gone? Back to Penleven, she suspected, to lick his wounds and brood upon a woman who lacked both principles and sense.

Even now she blushed at the memory of her wantonness.

Twenty-two and she had known the pleasures of the flesh only twice. If the reality had not been so tragic, it could have almost been funny.

But at least Thomas was safe. She put her hand into his, liking the feeling of closeness.

He had had absolutely no idea as to who had abducted him, but had escaped from the small cottage he had been incarcerated in after two days of isolation.

The perpetrators had not come back, and, after crouching in the undergrowth for half a morning to see if they might materialise, he had returned to Campton to find the Earl of Hilverton and his wife about to leave for Exeter.

'If only you had come back to Exeter on your own to find me,' she said softly and her brother looked at her, surprised.

'No one would have known about us then.'

'I think we would have had to leave anyway, Caro. The de Lerins,' he clarified when she looked up, confused. 'They have obviously found out where we live.'

'Why did they not kill you then or at least haul you up before the judiciary? Why just leave you there? Why take such a chance on escape? And no note of intent either.'

'Perhaps someone scared them off?'

'Who?'

'I don't know.' Tosh rubbed his nose and grimaced.

Both his eyes were now swollen and the skin across his cheeks was a violent yellow green.

'Does it hurt?'

'Not as badly as before.'

'I could get you a cold compress.'

'No, don't fuss.'

Sensing irritation, she left it at that and folded a pile of damp washing to lay out by the fire.

For the first time since she was young, life had ceased to delight her, the charade of being somebody she wasn't becoming increasingly intolerable.

To leave Campton with its green rolling hills and soft brambled lanes was distressing. To never walk the path again between this house and the big one or experience the kindness of those who knew her here.

Belonging.

Something she had never had before.

A place.

A home, with Alex raised not in the midst of strangers but with friends, raised exactly in the fashion that she herself had never been.

It was her fault. All her fault.

Wicked lust spoiled everything.

'No!'

Such an easy word to say and Thornton Lindsay would have listened had she had the backbone to say it. But she hadn't. Her own fulfilment had been paramount over everything, Alexander's happiness, Tosh's future, Gwenneth's friendship.

She had sacrificed all for an out-of-control libido.

She was ashamed. Deeply. The predicament they found themselves in again was all her fault. And her brother's magnanimous lack of accusation was not helping either.

'If we travelled towards the east, it might be safer.' Tosh was already laying out the map and tracing a path of travel with his finger.

'I've always thought Norwich might be a town that would be worth the visiting. It's out of the way of the regular London traffic and far enough into the countryside to be a long way from anywhere.'

Tears blurred her eyes. 'I don't know if I can do this any more…start again—'

She could tell he was losing patience with her when he butted in. 'What other option is there, then, Caroline?'

She thought of Alexander and shook her head.

'None.'

'Then let's get packing. If we can be ready to leave tomorrow, it will be better for everyone, and if I see Hilverton sniffing around here and looking at you like he was doing on the journey home, then I'll bloody well punch his head in. A devout man, my arse.'

Caroline smiled, her brother's humour dispersing the true ache of regret.

'Anna could keep all the bigger things. She is getting married in the middle of next year and could do with some furniture.'

'And Johnathon can have our books. He reads, you

know, even given his lack of education, and would appreciate them.'

The dissemination of their lives.

Again.

Rising from her chair, she walked into her bedroom on hearing the small waking sounds of her son. And her heart fell further when she saw that with every day he began to look more and more like his father.

Thornton frowned as he read the letter that had arrived in the morning post.

The insignia of the Earl of Ross was vaguely familiar; slitting the flap open with his paper knife, he began to read. His shout brought his secretary into the room at full tilt.

'Is there a problem, Your Grace?'

'Do you know anything at all about the Earl of Ross and his daughter?'

James reddened considerably, giving Thornton his answer.

'The Earl wrote while you were ill, sir, demanding an immediate answer. When I asked you for a reply to his letter regarding a visit to Penleven with his family and daughter you gave me reason to think that the idea was a good one.'

'How?'

'How what, Your Grace?'

'How did I give you this…reason?'

'You did nothing to make me think that the visit of a woman known for her virtue and piety would be counteractive to your own good well being.'

'I was unconscious.'

'I beg to differ, Your Grace. At one point you seemed much recovered and it was then that I broached the subject.'

'I see.'

'I have heard much about this particular lady, you understand, and the thing that strikes me above all else is her ability to make others happy. She has an easy nature and is seldom at odds with anybody.'

'A sterling attribute, indeed.' His tone decried that he thought anything but. 'She will be visiting us early next week as her family are travelling through these parts and it seems we have been chosen as a...convenient stopover.'

'Then I will inform the housekeeper of the dates, sir, if you could supply me with the numbers.'

'Very well.'

He handed over the letter, though as his secretary walked to the door he stopped him.

'And, James...'

'Yes, sir?'

'I would prefer to hand out these sort of invitations myself in future.' Thornton heard the anger in his voice but could not, for the life of him, soften his chastisement. After all, he was now stuck with a visitation he did not want and a father who was probably expecting a lot more than he was going to get.

'Very good, Your Grace.'

There was a low-tone whispering outside even as the door shut.

Henry, he presumed, and no doubt in on the scam. If they were less like family he would have had no compunction in dismissing them on the spot, but James's family had served the Lindsays since time immemorial, and the clumsy attempt at matchmaking would have been done with the best of intentions.

Thornton's arm hurt, his eyes ached, and the memory of Caroline wrapped protectively around her twin brother in the room in Exeter infuriated him.

Five days ago he had never wanted to see her again. And yet now he knew that he could not just leave things as they were. He wanted to understand what it was that kept her so firmly in his mind, the feel of her body against his soft and pliant, her midnight blue eyes locked into his own.

When he lifted the second letter from the pile he frowned. Gwenneth Hilverton's letter was full of eloquence, describing Caroline Weatherby's current position in every detail, the village gossip, the local priest's sermon, shopkeepers withholding their goods and their upcoming departure from a home that they had known for well over a year.

And blaming him in that peculiarly careful way that well brought-up women had of expressing opinion.

Anger surfaced as Thornton balanced leaving things exactly as they were against the odds that the child could actually be his. Lord. Could he leave Caroline to the mercy of circumstance when his part in all of this had been every bit as culpable as her own? More, perhaps, given the cold calculation of their meeting. And if she was the mother of his child… Had he actually ever doubted it?

'James.'

His secretary came back, wariness in his eyes and a hint of sullenness.

'I want you to organise a coach to Campton and bring Mrs Weatherby, her son and brother back to Penleven.'

He could give them shelter for at least a while. He had had dealings with what it was like to be an outcast before, and if others thought that she was now easy game…

'And, James…'

'Yes, Your Grace?'

'Make certain that you don't take no for an answer.'

Caroline heaved the last of her few clothes into an old trunk and folded Alex's blankets and bedding across the top. In their past sixteen months they had acquired ten times as much as they ever had before and she was at a loss as to what now to get rid of and what to take.

The toys and books others had gifted to Alexander were ones that he would grow to cherish and love and her new gardening tools could certainly be used in the next house. Her paints were also too valuable to just give away and she hoped that perhaps she could continue bringing in money with her portraits.

Wiping her hand across her brow, she tightened the mob cap around her head and bent to the task of sorting, smiling at Alexander next to her as he reached out for a doll Gwenneth had brought him only two weeks prior.

A soldier boy doll, his knitted jacket scarlet red. What had Thornton Lindsay worn, she wondered, as he had crossed Europe under orders from the King? She had heard stories of intelligence officers being summarily executed by the enemy when caught out of uniform and incognito. A dangerous life of extremes. He still wore secrecy and distance like a cloak and she found herself imagining how difficult it must be to just come back…and fit in.

Tosh's shout had her standing and her eyes were caught by the sight of a coach rounding the corner and coming to rest outside their gate. A coach with an insignia.

Endure forte was written in gold and red across the helm of a knight in armour.

The Lindsay coat of arms! Her heart raced as fear, hope and dismay coursed through her, and Alex, reacting to her alarm, began to howl. She would not go out there! She would not meet the Duke of Penborne dressed like this, looking like this. Her hand snatched the cap from her head and she straightened her skirts, angry at herself for even thinking such considerations important, and watching as Tosh spoke with a small dark-haired servant who had alighted from the coach.

Perhaps Lindsay had not come at all. The windows were dressed in thick velour, sheltering prying eyes from any inside inhabitants, and she could detect no twitching of the curtains.

When Tosh turned to come inside she tried to read the expression on his face.

'You have no idea what has just happened, Caro,' he began even before he had crossed through the door's lintel. 'The Duke has invited us to stay at Penleven and his man said he would be in severe difficulty should he not be able to persuade us to accompany him back.'

'I do not know… Is he there?'

'Lindsay? No. I didn't see him, at least.' He stopped to peer out of the window and began to shake his head. 'I doubt he would just hide inside, do you?'

'Go out and see.'

Tosh's answering frown was heavy. 'We have little money, Caroline, a small baby and lots of luggage. Outside lies a means of transport, two men to help us lift our possessions and the chance to reach the south coast without parting with a penny.'

'You're saying you think we should accept the offer but get out before we reach his lands?'

He drew his hand through his hair and swore. 'I no longer know what to think, Caro. At Exeter I tried to kill

Lindsay for what he had done to you, but I can see in your eyes that things aren't as simple as they would appear.'

'He is Alexander's father, Tosh.'

'He is also the man who will never marry you, Caro.'

'But if I just leave...without knowing...without trying...'

He began to laugh. 'The Lord moves in mysterious ways. "O my God I trust in thee; let me not be ashamed, let not mine enemies triumph over me." I looked up Malcolm's quote and found it was from Psalms 24. Mine is Psalms 25. Perhaps there is a message in it. I, for one, think we should see just where this invitation takes us.'

He smiled as she reached out and took his hand. Penleven. She imagined the castle repelling a thousand years of enemies. Lord, once they were inside such a place they need never fear anyone again, save for the lord who owned it, walking his corridors in isolation and reclusion. Why would he want her there? Them there? A worm of promise turned and she quickly stamped it down—she could not afford the luxury of groundless hope around a man like Thornton Lindsay.

And survive.

Chapter Eleven

They had been on the road now for hours and the storm that whipped at the coach as it travelled towards Penleven showed no signs at all of letting up.

Trapped within a velvet cocoon that was transporting them ever closer towards a man who had ruined her. The thunder outside made her jump as she looked across at her brother, fast asleep on his side of the seat, the bruises faded now to a light lemon colour and strange against the gilt blond of his hair. Tears pricked at the back of her eyes. For him. For her. For Alex tucked up in his little basket at her feet. A small family with no home and no past, hurtling through a rainswept dusk to no future.

A movement outside made her turn to the window. Wiping the condensation from the glass, she saw a lone rider, effortless in his movements and hair loose in the gathering wind. Wild. Dangerous.

Thornton Lindsay. She knew it was him even before the flash of lightning lit up his face, runnels of water on the hard planes of his scarred cheek.

And yet the carriage did not slow, did not stop, did not veer at all from its course as the darkness swallowed him up, lost in the tempest.

Had she imagined him there, her mind playing tricks on what she would have wanted to happen?

Placing her fingers upon her throat, she felt the moisture from the glass trickle down the valley between her breasts and, sensing a shiver up her spine, she closed her eyes and slept.

They arrived at the castle well into the night and an icy blast from the north filled her cloak as they stepped from the coach.

Everything was cold. Her feet, her hands, her face. Wrapping Alexander close, she tried to infuse into him what little heat she still had as she looked around.

Penleven stood against a cloud-whipped sky, a fortress on the edge of the sea itself, she thought, the voice of waves high pitched as they beached themselves against cliffs.

Penleven.

Alexander's lost heritage. She wondered again as to why they had been asked here and came up with no answers.

'Welcome to Cornwall, ma'am.' The man she had

seen from the cottage window at Campton was beside her, soaked despite a heavy oilskin coat and hat, and the driver behind him made her look twice.

Twins.

She was certain they were twins. Her heart warmed and she laid her hand upon his arm.

'Thank you. I hope you will now both have the chance to get dry.'

Surprise laced his eyes. 'We will, ma'am. Now if you'd go with the housekeeper, she will see you inside to your rooms and out of this weather.'

A line of servants held large umbrellas over the disembarking party, the rain softer now and easing. Caroline folded a blanket across the head of Alex and watched as Tosh lifted his basket.

Where was Thornton Lindsay? she wondered, glancing down the manicured driveway to make certain that no single rider trailed in, but only the rain slanted across the track, the leaves of trees blown in eddies of wind, dark against the light of the moon.

Plastering a careful smile upon her lips, she followed the housekeeper and the lesser servants inside. Perhaps he would not come at all. Perhaps he truly did not care. Exeter after all had taught her that, for the Duke had disappeared the moment after their lovemaking and had made no contact in person since. Eight days ago now. And almost nine. She hated the way her mind could calculate exactly what her soul did not want to know, hated the fact that sorrow could take such a hold of joy and wrench the very gladness from her bones.

An old woman dressed in black stood in the portico, her hair severely tied back and a look that was hardly happy in small dark eyes.

'So ye'd be the woman my grandson has been telling me of.' The accent of Scotland was well imbued into her words. 'And this is the child?'

Before Caroline could stop her, the woman pushed back the blanket and bony fingers caressed the side of her son's chubby cheek. 'A bonny wee lad to be sure, but a Lindsay?' There was a strong sense of challenge at the end of her question, and a decided crusty impatience. 'I am the Duchess of Penborne and Thorn asked me here to act as a chaperon whilst you are visiting.'

Thornton's grandmother!

Feeling it appropriate, Caroline curtsied and introduced her brother. 'It is very good to meet you, Your Grace, and we thank you for your hospitality.'

'Do you indeed, Mrs Weatherby? Penborne Castle must be a far cry from your cottage in Campton.'

The question was said in such a way that Caroline was at pains as to know how to answer it. Was the old woman implying a lack of breeding, or, worse, was she hinting that she felt their presence here smacked of gold digging? Uncertain, she merely smiled.

Thomas, however, seemed completely unaware of any tension and jumped into the growing gap of silence.

'I have always wanted to visit Scotland, Your Grace, and see the places spoken of in the poems of Robbie Burns. "Let other poets raise a fracas, 'Bout vines an' wines...an' stories wrack us..."'

'From Rabbie's "Scotch Drink", I'd wager?' The old Duchess waited till he nodded before continuing, her curiosity overcoming frostiness. 'Did ye learn that as a wee bairn?'

'No. I learned that on a card table in Antwerp. The Scottish fellow I was playing found his concentration much improved when reciting a good dollop of poetry. And the strange thing was that I did too after I beat him.'

'You were a card player?'

'And a good one, too.'

When Thornton Lindsay's grandmother laughed, Caroline saw, for the first time, the ghost of a woman who must have once been breathtakingly beautiful. Perhaps she had judged her too hastily, she thought. There was little time to dwell upon any of it, however, as the housekeeper shepherded them through to the first floor and to their adjoining rooms, leaving them with the promise of a hot meal delivered on a tray as soon as their luggage had been seen to.

Her room was decorated in cream and white and the bed was the largest she had ever seen. Even the staterooms at Malmaison had not been as impressive or as comfortable. A roaring fire blazed in a grate that stretched across an entire wall and, to one side by the window, a sofa and two chairs were placed before a generous oaken table.

She laid Alexander down on the bed, bolstering pillows around him so that he would not fall, and placed her bag on a wooden chest. A knock at the door had her turning and the housekeeper entered, pushing a cot with two wheels at one end.

'We thought that you might need this, ma'am. It was the Duke's when he was a little baby and his father's before then. There are more blankets should you want them.'

'I am sure that this will be perfect.' Her fingers ran across the wool of the covers, and the lawn of tiny embroidered sheets. Thornton Lindsay had slept here as a baby. The fact intrigued and delighted her, though as she shut the door behind the departing housekeeper she wondered who the 'we' she spoke of was. The Duchess or the Duke himself? Lifting Alexander up, she removed the top layer of his clothing and placed him carefully in the cot, smiling as he reached out to the colourful embroidery along the side.

'Do you like it, darling?' she crooned and bent to kiss him on the cheek just as her brother came into her room.

'They seem well prepared for a baby,' he commented and sat down in one of the armchairs by the fire.

'It was Thornton Lindsay's.'

'Lord.'

His sigh was so heartfelt that Caroline frowned.

'I hope that the Duke understands that you are not

the fair game you were in London. If he beds you and expects to—'

'We have had this talk before, Tosh.'

'And will do so again, Caroline.'

'Thornton Lindsay is Alexander's father and you promised me you would not say anything at all about what has happened before, that you would let me deal with this situation as I saw fit.'

'I hope that was not a rash promise.' His winsome smile defused the tension and he shrugged his shoulders and leant back. 'I wonder where Lindsay is? Perhaps he is away?'

Caroline thought of the dark shadow-rider chasing rain and wind and carriage and shook her head.

'He is here.' Her spirits sank even as she said it, for she could feel that he was, in the soft recesses of her own heart.

A noise awakened her, barely the whisper of a footprint in her room. Staying perfectly still to gauge the threat, she saw Thornton Lindsay standing next to the cot, his hands drawn tight across the wooden rails, moonlight from the opened curtains falling across him.

He did not touch, did not reach out, did not lay even a finger against the shape that was his son, but in the lack of movement Caroline saw something that was far more all consuming and passionate. His face burned with desperation and want and the muscles along the line of his cheek were taut with longing.

For his child.

For Alexander.

For family.

She knew exactly how it was he was feeling because in the first moment of his life when Alexander had been placed into her waiting arms she had felt it too.

A parent.

A place in the world measured neither in wealth nor knowledge nor position, but simply by love.

When a single tear fell from her cheek into the softness of the pillow, he turned.

'You are awake?'

Caroline saw how he stepped back from the cot and brought his hands behind him, saw the mask of indifference fall like a shutter over amber eyes. She barely knew how to answer and the fact that she wore only a very thin nightgown made it even more difficult again. She could not sit up, could not meet his glance as she would have liked to, head on and direct.

'Was it you on the horse?'

A ridiculous question and no way to begin any sort of conversation, but then this whole situation was absurd.

He made no answer as he changed the subject altogether.

'He looks like me. What colour are his eyes?'

'A lighter shade of your own.'

'I see.' He nodded his head and drew one hand through his hair. In worry. In bafflement. In the sheer and huge responsibility of offspring. Caroline knew that feeling too and hurried into an explanation.

'I never knew who my own father was…' She stopped and tried to rein in a surprising anger. 'I am glad it will not be the same for Alexander.'

'And you are certain that he is mine?'

The words cut her to the quick, but she kept her face perfectly impassive.

'You said yourself that he looks like—'

He gave no credence to her argument, but interrupted easily. 'If I were to claim this baby as my own, how many other men might come forward to challenge me on the fact?'

Caroline felt the hard punch of betrayal wind her. He had not asked her to Penleven for a truce or a tryst. He had not asked her here to be his mistress, or for even a milder version of friendship. He had brought her here to determine whether this child was indeed his son.

Fright made her shake.

If he were to ascertain such a thing, how far was he likely to go to make sure that Alex stayed in Cornwall?

Any length!

For the first time since being in the company of Thornton Lindsay she felt fear. Bone-deep fear. The kind that kept her mute and clammy.

And his anger-laced eyes were leached by wariness.

'I see.' He turned away and then turned back. 'I asked

you once before for the truth of your name, Caroline. Are you now ready to give it to me? For this child's sake?'

'I do not understand…'

'Disguises have a way of tearing the heart out of honesty. If he is mine and you do not allow him the protection of my title, how in the hell are you going to shield him? What happens when he is ten or twenty? When he has children of his own? Anstretton. Weatherby. Lindsay. The son of a widow or a harlot or a Duke?' His eyes settled on the bracelet on the small table next to her bed. 'Or a French woman with the surname of "St C"?'

She froze. Her bracelet. He had worked this out from a tiny inscription in gold? This time she could allow no question.

Thomas's safety or Alexander's?

A choice.

Give her son a home and her brother would die.

No choice at all.

She sat up and made certain that the sheets of the bed fell to her lap and was pleased when the dark glow of the fire danced in beguiling shadows across the full roundness of her breasts. Distraction. With the Duke as an adversary she needed all the help that she could muster.

'The child is not yours.'

'You are lying.'

'We will leave Penleven in the morning.'

'No.'

'You cannot stop us.'

'But I think that I can. Which sane person would question where this baby would be better placed? Penleven and stability, or a number of different addresses and masquerades? Do I need to go on?'

'No.'

'I thought not.'

He smiled and moved away. 'I would be seen as a father, Caroline, who is trying to protect his only child. What manner of man would allow his progeny to become a gypsy?' The amber in his eyes danced bright. Bitterly gold.

'And me? What will happen to me?'

He walked across to the bed and traced the line of one areola in a cold and dispassionate manner. 'You have bounteous charms that I am more than prepared to bargain for; a liaison will at least give you the opportunity to be close to Alexander.'

'And Thomas?'

'I could do with another manager.'

'I see.'

And she did. Saw just how neatly he had tied her up to a position she had previously refused, made her morals ludicrous and pointless things with the neck of her son and her twin brother at stake.

The Heartless Duke.

She remembered his *nom de plume* and tears flooded into her eyes.

'For how long?'

'When I find a wife, you will be installed in a house in the village.'

'And forgotten?'

For the first time he smiled. 'I am not certain that it would ever be possible to forget you.'

When his hand fell lower to cup her breast she looked up. Fully dressed with his hair falling across the whiteness of a snowy cravat, his harnessed sexuality was completely evident. She felt the heat of want blush her cheek. Saw it too in his face, the muscles of his jaw grinding tense.

'It is not a fight I want, Caroline.'

'Then let me go.'

'I can't…'

His voice broke on the admission and he laid back the sheets, carefully looking at her. She felt the cold rush of air and the warmer touch of his fingers. Lower. Lower. And when he stood a few minutes later to remove his clothes she merely opened her arms and waited.

When she awoke he was gone. And the shadows that wreathed the room were heavy.

Like her heart!

She was a mistress: a woman who could be taken whenever and wherever her protector should demand it. A fallen woman like her mother, existing on the crumbs of rich men for survival. Her hand wandered to the wetness between her legs. She had not even taken precaution against conception! Another child.

'When I find a wife, you will be installed in a house in the village.'

Her hand came up to her mouth and she felt the hot tears of self-loathing spill across it, a noise from the cradle opposite keeping her cries silent.

She was trapped, here at Penleven, caught in a role of her own making.

Her mind began to spin as she thought back. Back to the heady days of Malmaison when Napoleon had rejected Josephine for another. With stealth and wit Madame de Beauharnais had stalked him, bringing the general back into the shelter of her arms, indiscretions and alliances forgotten under the onslaught of what was truly theirs.

Could she do the same?

How far apart were the emotions of lust and love? Thornton was judicious in his movements, vigilant with his words and his time. He had not stayed in bed after they had made love, had not tarried to be woken in the morning with her beside him and had, even in the final heat of lovemaking, held some part of himself back, some important part. And that was the part of him that she so desperately needed.

What could she use to bring him to a point of no return?

She wiped her tear-wet hands against the sheet on the bed and rose to look out of the window, the moonlight bright now on the lands around the castle. Her ears picked up the sound of her brother snoring in the next room and of her son in his beautiful new cot as he turned to find comfort.

At least they were safe behind the ramparts of Penleven, well fed and warm and with a gap of time that offered them shelter should she do what was expected of her.

Thornton walked to the cliffs, walked to the very edge of the world before the land fell away into the boiling white cauldron of sea and was lost into nothingness.

The child is not yours. We will leave Penleven in the morning.

Not his, when he could see the mark of his father on the small white face and his father and his father's father, stamped with the particular features of a thousand years of Lindsay lineage.

Not his!

Not his?

Caroline Anstretton/Weatherby made him furious, made him careless, made the familiar dulling ennui vanish into either a fathomless lust or an unending wrath.

He could not believe how he let her bait him, how he rose to the lure of her breasts in the firelight like a green and untried boy, all brawn and no brain.

Stooping to pick up a rock by his feet, he threw it with his full force out into the darkness of sky. God. He had even threatened her whilst demanding his rights as her lover in exactly the same sentence.

Was he stupid?

She made him so.

She did not trust him, that much was certain—and to be honest, how was it possible for him to even be thinking of trusting her?

He should let them all go: her and her brother and the son with the eyes in a lighter shade than his own. He should take a wife and start a family that was truly his, and far from the deceit, chaos and illusion that Caroline Anstretton seemed for ever fond of. He should toss her out of Penleven with a hefty purse and forget her.

And yet here he was, blackmailing her into staying, and following the carriage on a wild and rainy night from the north coast to the south just to make certain that she did not get out, did not disappear.

He smiled at himself and turned the signet ring that he wore on his little finger around and around.

Circles.

Life came in circles when you thought about it.

Lost. Found. Happy. Sad. Lonely.

Content.

The small bud of it warmed his heart and blossomed into an almost ache.

He could not lose her.

Not again.

Not even when she looked him straight in the eyes

and denied the child was his. Not even when the tears that filled her eyes magnified dark blue orbs of hate.

His mistress. Caroline.

For now, at least, that would just have to be enough.

Chapter Twelve

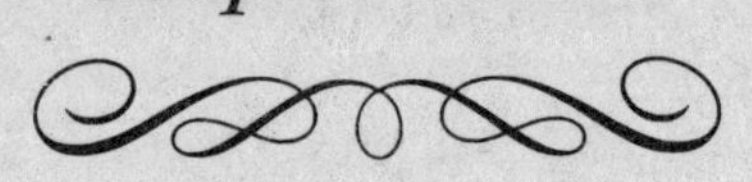

Breakfast was set out in a downstairs salon, the sideboard filled with as much food as they usually consumed in a whole week at Campton. She marvelled at the waste of it all and smiled as Tosh sat beside her, his plate filled with every conceivable thing on offer.

'You are not eating, Caro?'

Sipping her tea, she tried to push down nervousness, a noise startling her as the Duke entered the room.

'Good morning. Welcome to my castle. I hope you are both comfortable.'

Today the stubble on his chin was dark and he wore his patch. And in his eye, when it caught her own, there was something akin to guilt.

'If there is anything you should require, you just need to ask my housekeeper. Whatever you need shall be provided.'

When Tosh stood she held her breath. Last time he had seen the Duke of Penborne he had been trying to knock his head off and the situation here seemed slightly ludicrous. Good manners had her brother holding out his hand and Caroline was pleased when Thornton took it. She did not need the extra worry of retaliation for perceived wrong and in all honesty that awful scene in Exeter had been as much her doing as it had the Duke's.

'Your nose looks a lot better.'

'I could say the same of your arm, Your Grace.'

The air between the men bristled with unsaid accusations, an uneasy truce brought about by circumstance.

With real consternation she pushed back her own seat and stood. 'It would be most appreciated if you could find my brother a position on one of your farms, Your Grace. A good position.'

Tosh turned to look at her in utter disbelief.

But Caroline merely smiled. Two could play at the game the Duke had set out and she had fulfilled her part of the bargain more than amply last night.

She lifted her chin and looked him straight in the eye, and as the moment lengthened the Duke of Penborne dismissed his servants to a further distance with a quick gesture.

'How is it you know Adele Halstead? I would prefer the…truth.' He left a slight gap between the words, giving the question an edge of danger.

No mincing words, then! No careful circling around honesty.

'We met her in Paris. She lived there for a time when our mother was still alive.' Not completely a lie.

'Your mother?'

'Eloise St Clair.'

There was a silence. Caroline could almost see the way Thornton Lindsay was putting together the fragmented facts into a cohesive whole. And knew the second that the name of her mother truly registered.

'The infamous daughter of the Reverend who ran off alone to Europe?' An unexpected humour laced his words. 'Lord, she was your mother?'

He waited as she nodded.

'I see.'

'She was not as people in England said that she was.' Caroline hated the anger she could hear in her voice and for the second time that day she bit her tongue hard, wondering what it was in him that made her want to explain.

'No?'

'No. She was a woman who found the strictures of life difficult.'

'How old were you when she died?'

'Seventeen. We were seventeen.'

'And had you always lived in France?'

Looking across at Thomas, she shook her head. 'We lived in other places too.'

'With her?'

'Not always.'

'But together?'

'Yes.'

'And your father?'

Silence.

'Are you interested in farm management, Thomas?'

The quick change in subject had Caroline reeling. A few short questions and the Duke of Penborne had found out more about their lives than anyone ever had before. Their loneliness. Their uncertainty. Their togetherness. Their lack of family. And now he would offer her brother the chance of work that could see him self-sufficient and eminently respectable? She watched the slow blush of excitement tinge Tosh's cheeks.

'I am, Your Grace.'

'Then perhaps you could accompany me on the rounds of Penleven later today and we could talk.'

'I would very much like that.'

'If you have finished breakfast, my secretary could show you the boundaries of the estate on a map in the library.'

When he was gone, Caroline took a breath. Left alone, the familiar pull was stronger, like magnets straining against opposite poles. She stepped back a little. Embarrassed. Breathless. Almost nervous.

'Thank you for helping my brother, Your Grace.'

'One promise for another, Caroline. Is it Weatherby

or Anstretton I should be placing on any legal contract with him?'

'St Clair would be more correct. Though I would prefer to be known here as Mrs Weatherby.'

His eye brushed across the inscription on her bracelet. 'I shall be taking a short drive around the hills of Penleven in an hour. Would you and Alexander like to accompany me?'

He did not touch her, did not move forward, did not in any way allude to the sensuality of last night, and yet in his eye she saw the burning promise of what was always between them.

Heat. Fierce and incandescent. Unstoppable. The throbbing want of him unbalancing her anger, replacing the risk of it all with hope. Hope of making things different.

When she nodded he turned and left and she realised that he had eaten nothing and that the large plates of eggs and bacon and toast had remained untouched.

She had dressed carefully in a dark brown coat and matching dress, a froth of lace at the collar and a cameo of her mother's pinned on top of it.

Alexander cooed on her lap as the coach trotted out of Penleven, his eyelashes dark against rosy cheeks and his hands grasping at the gold catch on the door.

A happy family going on a jaunt into town? How appearances could fool. Three people. A mistress, a man who was in the process of acquiring a proper wife and his unwanted bastard son.

Pushing down ire, she tried to rally, but today, with last night's sleepless worry pulling at her, she found that she just could not.

Thornton, on the other hand, was in the best of moods as he pointed out a river and the local hills and a cave that he had sheltered in with his brother when he was younger.

'You have a brother?' She had seen no sign of any family save the old grandmother.

'He died young of scarlet fever. My mother and father caught it too and passed away a few days after him.'

'Who cared for you?'

'I was at Eton.'

'And at term's end?'

'I stayed there.'

Challenge was plainly scrawled across his face when she looked up. The scarring on his left cheek in this light was easily seen, the skin pulling at the edge of his eye in a way that she had not noticed before. Perhaps that was why he wore the patch. She longed to ask him about the explosion in the church, but did not dare to because of the questions that he might ask her back. When the carriage jolted she felt the length of his arm against her own and moved away quickly, tense in her reaction to such a tiny contact.

Stupid. Stupid. Stupid. She chided herself firmly,

making herself relax and smile. Her teeth gritted together as she did so, the muscles in her cheek protesting the staunchness.

'I would not think to send a small child far away to school even if it was the vogue to do so.' Here was a chance to install some of her philosophies of upbringing at least.

'Neither would I.'

'I would hope a nanny could be employed at first and then a tutor. One that was not harsh and one that I liked.'

'You do not believe in discipline?'

'Punishments benefit no one. Were you punished as a child?'

He pushed open the window next to him by releasing the leather catch. His hair moved in the wind and he deftly tied it back with a strap of leather he wore around his wrist. 'Eton was a school where retribution and penalty were art forms, and I was a worthy recipient, having no parents to ever complain about the bruising.'

'Why did you not live with your grandmother, then, after...?' She petered out.

'Morag had problems of her own at that time and could not also deal with mine. It is only more recently that she moved from Edinburgh to Plymouth. There...' He pointed as if he were tired of the personal nature of the conversation, and rapped on the top of the roof of the coach with his cane. 'This is what I wanted to show you.'

Sorrow consumed her and enlightenment. His childhood had been even lonelier than her own, a small abandoned boy who had grown up to be a man trusting nobody, patterns moulded in youth hard to shake in adulthood.

When the carriage slowed, he jumped out first and turned to help her.

'Could you take Alex?' she asked as she collected her reticule and lifted her skirts.

Uncertainty crossed into his eyes. 'I have not held a baby before—' His words stopped as she deposited Alexander into his arms and Caroline tried to hide a smile as he reached up to play with the Duke's snowy white cravat.

In the sunlight and close, the colour of their hair was exactly the same. Black night dark and slightly curly, almost touching as he leant downwards.

The spark of interest had taken. Alike. Alight. The flame of love would come whether he wanted it to or not. Already she saw how her tiny son watched him. When Thornton scratched his head Alex did the same, his nearly-words soft in the afternoon breeze.

'He speaks?'

'A few baby sounds that I recognise.'

'And walks.'

She smiled. 'He is only seven months. But he can sit now unaided.'

Information. She could see Thornton Lindsay storing it, remembering it, wanting to know what every father has since the very beginning of time.

Alex resisted as she tried to take him back, clinging on to his father with a surprising fervency, and when Thornton's hand came up telling her to leave him, she did.

'The place I want to show you is just here. My father built it for my mother.'

The cottage was beautiful, smothered in vines, a porch running the full length of the front and French doors placed to allow easy access from any point.

Walking up the small number of steps and on to the terrace, Caroline could see why the house had been positioned exactly where it was. A vista of hills and valleys and sea lay before her and far in the distance, through a stand of trees, Penleven jutted tall, the last bastion of human existence before the land fell into the sea below.

This cottage was all that the castle was not. Quiet. Calm. Peaceful. Simple.

A retreat.

'I can see why your mother would have loved it. Did she come here often?'

'Not as often as my father may have liked.' A peculiar tone lay in his words, giving Caroline the idea that there was more to this place than he was saying. When they went inside she saw what it was that he had not told her.

The house was just one single room with the biggest bed she had ever seen square in the middle. Draped in netting and heaped in pillows, she understood exactly his reason for bringing her here.

A love nest.

A mistress's lair.

Anger made her lash out. 'Do I have the right to ask you how often you plan to bed me, then? Now? This afternoon? This evening?'

'I will bed you when I want to, Caroline St Clair. Whenever and wherever I want to.'

Unexpectedly tears sprang. 'This may be a game to you…'

'A game. Ahh, but you have played me, sweetheart, as a master might. Your names. Disguises. Charades. This person. That person. Every time I have met you, you are completely different from the time before. And you tell me I am the one playing false.'

Sweetheart. He had called her sweetheart. It did not sound like a term he would often use and it had slipped out unconsciously. A beginning. Hope. Suddenly the world seemed like a brighter place to Caroline, a happier place, a place where perhaps in the unfolding scheme of things she might find sanctuary. With him.

The thought hit her hard, making her turn away to hide what she could so plainly feel in her eyes, on her face.

'Have you brought many others here?'

He did not answer.

'A wife might take exception to a mistress living so close.'

Still he said nothing.

'There is also the possibility to consider, I suppose, of other children conceived.'

'Enough, Caroline.' He took her hand and pulled her up close against him, the warmth of his body startling through the thickness of cloth. And for a moment she stood still, her son and her lover making a circle around happiness, their breaths against her skin offering the promise of something more. Something treasured. The sun was on their heads and the scattering clouds ran fast against the sea winds straight off the continent.

Home.

Safety.

An echo of something precious. When her fingers tightened against the breadth of his forearm he instantly pulled back.

'I think we should go.' The tone of his voice was reserved and formal as he shepherded her out and closed the doors behind them. Shut. Sealed. Secured against intrusion. Against the feeling of what had just been.

When Alexander began crying in earnest, she was glad, for she knew that the Duke of Penborne would not stay in their company for long.

He could not.

She was the daughter of a woman who had fled England in a scandal and one who had no notion of whom or where her father was. She owned nothing save a ruined reputation and a past that could never be told. She was like the perpetually unwelcomed wedding guest that Samuel Taylor Coleridge had spoken of in his poem about an ancient mariner: 'Alone, alone, all, all alone.'

With one child conceived out of wedlock, she could claim the pretence of widowhood. What if she were to fall pregnant again? And again? How long would it be before Tosh challenged Thornton over her honour? And lost?

Soon. Now, if he only knew.

Another secret.

This time from her twin brother, the last person in the world whom she would deceive. And if one of these men killed the other, how could she bear any of it?

She shook her head firmly and resolved to make certain of holding her confidences close. Perhaps if she encouraged Thornton to install her brother at Millington for a while, she could sort out what to say? The very thought of separation made her stomach sick, but to keep Tosh safe she would be prepared to do anything.

Anything.

Even lie with a man night after night in the hope that love might blossom, and smile as if she did not nurse even a care in the world when she met him the next morning.

Thornton sat in his library, watching the dying moments of a candle flicker in front of him.

Three o'clock.

All he wanted to do was to take Caroline St Clair into his arms and lose himself in her very warmth.

Lord. He worried about the way she was reeling him in. Her smile. Her voice. Her easy laughter and unexpected tears. Always there had been a part of him that had remained…his…in any relationship. Even with Lilly there had been a distance, a place where he observed and calculated, where his heart did not quite follow into the deep watches of night. He had maintained a coldness that with Caroline he could feel the first thawing of.

A few days she had been at Penleven and he was desperate to be with her as soon as the darkness fell, as soon as the candles were lit, the ache of his want standing proud even here in the library. All he yearned to do was to take her. Quickly. To spill his seed. Without caution. Heedless. Deliberate. So unlike him! Desperate.

Dangerous.

Relax your guard and chaos would follow. How often in his life had he learned that lesson? When he had shown her the cottage on the estate it had been in his mind to tell her that this was where he had thought she could live. But he had not. Why not? Why had he not laid down the ground rules of a relationship that could never be…sustainable?

He swore and sighed.

Because he could not hurt her. Because in the depths of her midnight blue eyes he saw a vulnerability that broke the resolution of his intent and made him want to…cherish her, make things easier for her, to take the worries of the world from her face and provide a sanctuary.

Lord, the very idea of such altruism concerning a mistress made him smile and he was laughing at his own questionable reasoning when a letter to one side of his desk attracted his attention. The Earl of Ross would be arriving tomorrow with his family. And his daughter. He groaned and threw the letter into the fire where it caught immediately and went up in a welter of flame. Why the hell had he let himself be talked into this proposition? Why had he not followed his initial instinct and cancelled the visit completely?

He did not want a wife.

He wanted Caroline.

He did not want a happy guileless girl.

He wanted Caroline. Full-fleshed and mysterious. Complex. Sensual. The mother of his child. Children. More than one? He wanted to see her belly swollen with his seed, her full breasts round and ripe. He had missed out on that once and would not again.

His mistress.

To take.

Throwing back a stiff brandy, he cursed at the power she was exerting over him and resolved to take a step back. In sheer self-protection.

The sound of voices made Caroline tense. Laughter. Gossip. Children. When she rounded the corner of the blue salon, she saw the place filled with people, a beautiful girl on the sofa next to the Duke of Penborne.

Thomas was watching them from a chair at one end of the room and it was to his side that she went. There had been no talk of visitors, no preparation that a whole family was to descend on Penleven. She tipped her head when the men stood at her arrival, glad when she could sit down as Tosh vacated the armchair and stood behind her.

'The Earl of Ross and his daughter Jennifer will be with us for a few days, Mrs Weatherby.'

When all the gawping faces turned her way she was at a loss as to what to say about her own presence here, although the Duke solved the problem for her.

'Caroline and her brother are old acquaintances. They arrived earlier this week from London with my grandmother.'

'And a long journey it is too, Mrs Weatherby.' The Earl of Ross was a large red-faced man with a generous nose. His poor looks, however, had not been passed at all to his daughter, an amber-tressed beauty with lightly freckled luminous skin. 'Have you visited Cornwall often before?'

When the Duke said yes and she said no, there was a small moment of tension. Sitting back, Caroline let Thornton extricate her from the difficulty, for it was his lie after all.

The eyes of the young woman next to him were fixed on his face, on his cheek, on his ruined cheek, the slight frown marring her beautiful countenance suggesting that she had had no prior knowledge of any injury and was rather disconcerted by the discovery.

Did she not realise how rude she was being, how very tactless?

'Will you be staying in this part of the country for long, Lady Jennifer?' Perhaps a question could distract her from such an inconsiderate observance.

Vacuous eyes raked across her own. 'We will be in these climes for a fortnight with my cousins and I love Cornwall.'

Her father chuckled as he turned to the Duke of Penborne. 'We always remark on her interest, Your Grace. Every year we do the same. Some predestined fate, according to her aunt, who has the reputation of being something of a seer.'

'Indeed.'

There was barely a note of interest in Thornton Lindsay's voice as he gestured to the butler to proceed with the tea, though it did not seem to put the Earl of Ross off his stride at all.

'Jennifer is also a prodigiously good piano player and I see you have a particularly fine piano, Your Grace?'

The question quivered in the air, and for a moment Caroline thought that the Duke would ignore the implication altogether.

'Please feel free to give us a tune, Lady Jennifer,' he finally said and Lady Ross clapped her hands and leaned forward.

'Oh, do, Jenny. Do play us something, dear.'

Jennifer's smaller sisters and brothers looked anything but happy when she rose and made much of adjusting her skirts and sitting at the piano. Her nails were so long that they almost raked the wood above the black and white keys, the ease of her position and life evident in the soft milky whiteness of her hands. Looking surreptitiously down at her own, Caroline frowned at the contrast. Short nails with the pigment of paint still residing in some of them and calluses on her first fingers where she had scrubbed Alex's clothes clean last week in boiling hot water.

She buried her fingers into her cotton skirt, angry at herself for even thinking such things important and resolving to enjoy herself.

The music that followed was like nothing Caroline had ever heard, though she was hardly an expert in anything musical. When she looked across at her brother she almost laughed at his face, which showed amazement crossed with an effort not to grimace. Thornton Lindsay sat implacably still, no expression at all giving any indication of his true feelings. Like the master spy he had been, she thought, and watched him. When his eyes caught hers they were carefully bland before he looked away. She wondered what he would have seen in her own.

The final flourish of Jennifer's rendition of a Mozart tune was greeted with loud claps from her mother and father and more polite accolades from Thornton and Thomas and herself.

Jennifer's father slapped his hands on his thighs as he stood more than proudly. 'She is our delight and joy, this young woman. Whoever marries her will be the luckiest fellow alive.'

His daughter beamed, the smile an exact copy of her mother's, and sat down even closer to the Duke of Penborne. Success had buoyed her confidence and she smacked his arm playfully as he said how interesting he had found her interpretation of the Mozart classic. Her parents watched the couple on the sofa with an ever-increasing felicity.

'Do you ride, Lady Jennifer?' Tosh's question was phrased more in politeness than in any true interest.

'I do, sir. My father taught me when I was young and we go to our country seat in Kent every summer.'

'She rides a horse as well as she plays the piano,' her father put in and his wife's laughter trilled around the room.

'Quite an accomplishment, then.' Something akin to abhorrence was just audible in Thornton Lindsay's voice, and when a message came for him he made much of the contents and excused himself summarily from the room.

The Ross girl sat pouting on the empty sofa, sullen pique written all over her. Her mother, trying to placate her, leaned over to pat her hand, but she flung it away and stood.

'I want to go back to my room now. I am tired.'

In less than five seconds the whole salon was emptied and Tosh and Caroline sat across from each other in a state of sheer disbelief.

'I would not wish her on my worst enemy,' her brother said when he had had time to recover his voice.

And they both began to laugh.

Alexander was fretful that evening, two new teeth cutting their way through swollen gums. As Caroline pondered a remedy for such a thing there was a knock on the door and the Duchess of Penborne walked in.

'I heard the child crying from outside on my way to bed. Are ye fine with him?'

'Thank you, yes.' She curtsied and waited until the older woman sat. 'Can I get you something, Your Grace?'

'Och, nay. 'Tis just that I heard the boy—'

An angry scream from Alex made her start and she was surprised when the old lady leant over and with strong hands plucked him out of her grasp.

'It's cold he'd be needing. The end of a bone against ice or a green twig from the oak tree. To bite on, you mind. It brings the teeth through quicker.'

Swollen gums clamped on an ancient finger and she smiled with an unhidden delight. 'It's been so long since I had a bairn on my lap, so long since the sound of children has rung through the halls of this place. I did not realise I missed it so.'

'Was Thornton an easy child?'

'He was always striving towards the next baby milestone, I recall. The first baby on the estate to walk by nine months, the fastest runner in the area before he went off to school. After that I did not see him so much.'

Why?

Why did you not bring your grandchild home and let each other heal your broken hearts? Why did you leave a child at a punitive and distant school and never find the time to claim him? Caroline longed to ask the questions. But she did not because already the old lady was standing and handing back her grizzly son.

'I will talk to the housekeeper tomorrow and have her bring ye something cold to soothe his gums. She is a competent woman with potions and well able to be trusted.'

'Thank you.' Cradling Alex, Caroline watched the old woman leave her room, feeling a small pleasure in the tone of their conversation. At least there could be a politeness between them, and she imagined she could learn much about the younger Thornton Lindsay from his grandmother, should she gain her confidence.

The Duke came before the clock had even struck ten fifteen. Earlier than usual and not alone.

'There is something I wish to speak to you about. The maid here will watch over Alexander while you are gone.'

The young woman curtsied. 'I have six brothers,

ma'am.' Her voice and smile were both kind. 'I promise you I will watch him well.'

As the woman settled herself, Caroline had little choice but to accompany the Duke as he left the room.

He led her down the corridor and up a flight of steep stairs to a chamber at the top of the tower. It was a library, the shelves of books around the room reaching to the ceiling, and subsisting of a substantial catalogue from what she could see at first glance.

'Why am I here, Your Grace?' Suddenly she was wary. Had he had enough of her already?

'We need to talk, Caroline. And I would prefer you call me by my given name. Thornton. Thorn if you should favour it.'

'Yes, sir...Thornton,' she amended when he looked at her sternly.

'I need your help.'

Of all the things she thought that he might have said, this was the very last of them. She stayed mute. Waiting.

'The Ross girl is proving annoyingly persistent and I hoped you might be able to be a foil.'

'A foil?' She could not quite keep amazement from her voice. Or her relief.

'An interested party, if you wish. A woman who would show some affection for me.'

'To deter Miss Ross?'

'Exactly.'

'I would have thought your personage enough to frighten even the most brave of young girls.'

'This one is proving surprisingly resilient and her parents' presence in the equation is not helping either. I should not wish to be trapped into a marriage I don't desire.' He pulled down a full bottle of brandy from a shelf behind him and, turning over two crystal glasses on a tray, poured out a generous measure in each. 'I found Miss Ross in my bedroom just before dinner. She said she had made the wrong turning and had come in by mistake. If my valet had not been with me…'

'You may have been attending your own wedding on the morrow?'

'I knew you would understand.'

She looked up sharply, a tone in his words that she did not quite fathom, the glint of amber surprisingly light.

Thornton smiled and finished his drink. Lord, her serious little face nearly undid him and the way she was now pacing up and down his library in thought made him want to snatch her to his side.

After a moment she turned back towards him, her mind seemingly made up. 'If I stayed near you and made certain that you were never alone in her company, would that help?'

'It would.' He tried his hardest to keep his words grave.

'My brother would not condone this, of course?'

'He won't know. He is due to leave for Holston after breakfast to look over some cattle.'

Nodding, Caroline chewed at a nail on her left hand. When Thornton looked closer, he saw each fingernail was indeed very short. She bit her nails. Often. The fact intrigued him.

'Did you have any plans in mind for the morrow?'

'I have promised the Ross party a ride around Penleven.'

'All of them?'

'Not the small children.'

'Well, with everyone there you should be safe?'

Thornton almost laughed, but stopped himself, liking the way Caroline counselled him. He had seen the way she had watched Jennifer Ross observe the scars on his face in the salon this afternoon and had tried to distract her from her rudeness. Did she think his feelings would be hurt somehow by such an exchange? Lord, he had spent over five years amongst men and women who would have had no compunction in murdering him were he to give them even half the chance and the last three ignoring the fascinated glances of well-meaning English folk when they comprehended the changes in his countenance.

Almost ten long years on the very edge of humanity and yet he was unsettled by the way Caroline now looked at him, concern on her face.

And care.

The Ross girl was of no threat to him whatsoever, but she did represent a way of keeping Caroline by his side and attentive within the company of others. And he needed her there! Beside him. Close.

He did not at this moment question the logic behind this deduction.

'You will promise not to allude in any way to the fact that I am your mistress?'

'I will.'

'Very well.' She held out her hand and he took it, warm and small in his, the gold bracelet catching the light of a candle, the warmth between them startling and distinct. 'Though if Jennifer Ross asks me questions about you it might be difficult, for we barely know each other.'

'I would beg to differ, Caroline,' he returned, suggestively raking his eyes across her body, and damping the smile that came as she snatched back her hand.

When she reddened dramatically, he tried to check his teasing. Lord, she had travelled Europe, carving a livelihood out of deceit, and yet she blushed in front of him like this? How the hell had she managed that? A slight uneasiness assailed him. Even when he thought he had the measure of her he did not.

He capitulated. 'What is it about me that you would like to know?'

'How did you become an intelligence officer under Wellington?'

'After Oxford I was at a loose end. Leonard had come back to stay at Penleven and was doing a good job of running the place and I was bored with country life. After expressing an interest in the army I sort of fell into it. At first I was a captain in Spain with Paget's Reserve Division and then I was seconded to Wellington as an intelligence officer.'

'And why did you stop?'

One hand scraped across the ridges of his left cheek. 'Part of the job of being a spy is to have the ability to blend in. After this I found that was difficult.'

All humour fled. 'Do you miss it?'

'At the time I cursed my bad luck, but returning to Cornwall was like a balm after all the years of uncertainty.'

'A balm.' She echoed his words.

She knew that feeling exactly. The hills had embraced her and the wild valleys had called her name. Her, an intruder with little claim to its beauty and a lifetime of homelessness. How must have he felt as heir of Penleven, with the march of his ancestors in the very bones of the earth and a solitude that protected completely?

'"Life marks the passage of our days." A woman in Paris told me that once not even a month after her husband had had his head blown off by cannon fire in the high hills of Corunna.'

'A brave acceptance. I was not quite so...acquiescent.'

'Of your scars?'

'They were the easiest things to bear,' he said quietly and moved back. Standing against the shelves of books in the half-light of his library, she drew in her breath.

'I have heard talk of a woman. Lillyanna?'

Real anger now masked his eyes and for the first time Caroline saw raw pain beneath the façade.

'There is always talk. The trick is to determine what is worth listening to.'

'And what isn't?' She knew he didn't wish for any further conversation, but whilst she had the chance she kept at it. 'I did not wish to pry…'

The clock behind suddenly boomed out the hour of eleven, startling them both.

Thorn placed his glass on the table. 'Stay with me.' His finger ran down the line of her jaw. 'Stay with me tonight, Caroline, and the maid will sit with Alex.'

'If Tosh found me with you and challenged you, would you fight him? If he got hurt because…'

'He won't.'

'You would promise?' She kept on at him because suddenly it was vitally important to her that she had his word.

'I promise.'

Breathing out, she felt her worry lighten even as she hated the red flush that marched across her cheeks and his answering lazy smile.

'If anyone else were to know…'

He circled behind and caught out at her hand, bringing the sensitive skin on the inside of her wrist up to the warmth of his mouth and holding it there.

Measuring the beat of her heart.

Pacing the moment in quiet.

And the amber strike of his velvet eyes up close was startling. Alive. Challenging.

'I think your last explanation to a packed court as to my sexual prowess was more damaging to your reputation than being my mistress could ever be.'

The thought made her grimace. 'I can never go back.'

'Oh, I don't know. London is notorious for its forgetfulness of scandal and yours, as a married woman, is not in the same league as the brutal deflowering of an innocent.'

Her pulse raced as she took in his words. A deflowered innocent. Her.

The hand that held her wrist brushed higher across the line of her bosom, cupping the round firmness and pulling at the lace overlay. And, further down, his leg came between hers, riding her loins on the rock of his thighs.

Hard. Meaningful. She shuddered as he took a husky intake of breath. And shuddered again as his thumb stroked her nipple into a proud rigidity. Her groan came involuntarily from the very depths of her stomach, an instinctual uncontrolled reflex of want. Primal. Elementary. Her head arched back, breath shallow against the knowledge of what his hands so easily could do to her body as fluid acquiescence overcame resistance.

Anywhere. Any time. Take me.

She no longer had the will to stop him. No longer the means to hold him at a distance, no matter how little she would receive in return.

An unequal giving. And she could not care. All she wanted was his hands on her body and his mouth at her breast and the final joining of flesh against flesh. Wet. Hot. Warm and melding. Release.

Love me, Thorn. Just me.

Please.

A single tear traced its way down her cheek and he stilled, his hands dropping away and an expression on his face that she had not seen there before.

'I promise I will not hurt you.'

Ambivalent hesitancy.

In a man who never faltered the emotion was more than surprising and when he moved back she let him, as much for her own well being as his. She had shown him too much of herself, and the ground beneath them had shifted somehow.

'But you do hurt me, Thornton, by keeping me here as your mistress.'

He frowned and pulled away, breaking contact. Now they were some place that words could not define, a watershed where decisions were needed to go forward. Or back.

But not tonight.

Not so soon.

Not when the feel of him bruised her with passion even as restraint was scrawled undisputedly on his face. The implacable distance that was his badge was back, lodged against sensuality in a hard band of need.

'I should really go. Alexander may have woken.' Shaky ground had the propensity to crumble at your feet after all and she had to be wary. For everyone's sake.

When he nodded she turned before he saw her disappointment. He would not come to her tonight. She knew it.

Thornton Lindsay, Wellington's most famous intelligence officer, needed to be in control, needed to fashion his existence in exactly the way he would want it. Tonight that had not happened. Tonight she had pierced a little place in the armour that held the world at bay.

The beginning of a true relationship?

She must take one step at a time, her brother protected by his promise and her son shielded by his name.

Like a phoenix, from the old rose the new. Better. Stronger. Real.

The banked fire in her room warmed her after the coldness of the passageway and she crossed to the cot beside her bed. Alex was fast asleep, as was the maid who watched over him. Gently tugging the woman's arm, she hushed away apologies and bade her find her own bed to sleep.

And then she sat in the wingchair by the fire and watched the sparks fasten themselves to the sooty back base of the grate.

Soldiers. Armies. Flaring. Dying. Small worlds within bigger ones, the flames of a piece of half-burnt wood catching and throwing orange shadows across everything. Outside the south-west wind howled against the castle, blowing straight in from the sea, and further afield, if she listened carefully, she could make out the sound of the waves hitting the land, long beaching rollers from the channel and beyond.

Home. Here. In the folds of Cornwall. In a countryside that had known peace for so long it was careless in its defences.

So different from Paris.

Her breath shallowed as she raised her hand up to the light from the fire, opening her fingers to warmth. Tears banked in her eyes for the goodness of this place, for the solid timelessness of it, for the durability of a castle built when the family name was young and for the love and laughter it must have known between then and now.

Permanence. She had not known how desperately she had wanted this until coming here. Coming home.

To Thornton Lindsay.

Chapter Thirteen

The ride across Penleven land was exhilarating. Seated on a horse that Thornton had chosen for her, Caroline felt a sense of freedom that she had never experienced before.

Shaking her head, she chased behind the Duke, his huge black horse exactly like the one she had seen from the carriage window on that first rain-filled night. The thought made her smile. It had been him then, racing against the wind and shepherding them towards his home. Why would he have done that if he truly did not care?

As they came to the top of a hill Thornton called a rest and waited for the Ross family to catch them up. Jennifer came first, her mouth slack with exhaustion and her face an unbecoming blotchy red. Her parents were only a few seconds behind her and all looked hopeful that this might indeed be the very end of the excursion.

'It's a beautiful land you live in, Lindsay.' The Earl of Ross's wife nodded diligently behind him as her husband gave the compliment. 'Our lands are, of course, as expansive, but this place has the sea beside it and there is something about the mix of green and blue.'

Jennifer pulled her mount over beside the big black and trilled with laughter as she slipped in the saddle, her arm grabbing at the Duke's in the process. 'The trail is rather testing, Your Grace. Perhaps I could ride home with you.'

Caroline had heard enough.

'Oh, do not give up on the joy of riding, Lady Jennifer. I did so once when I fell off my pony as a youngster and it took me all of three years to gather the nerve to again mount a horse. No. No. You must let me lend you some assistance, and follow my lead. Would that be all right with you, Thorn?' she added and gave him a beaming and intimate smile. 'I remember when I was a novice all those years ago and you allowed me to ride beside you when I was afraid.'

The use of his Christian name did not go unnoticed. 'You have known each other for a long time, then?' Lady Ross's voice was cold, the edge of displeasure at Caroline's meddling plainly audible.

'Oh, for ever.' The laugh that accompanied the words rang across the glade below them, and when she caught the eye of the Duke of Penborne upon her, she smiled. Broadly. 'When we were younger we made a pact that one day we would marry each other and live happily ever after.'

'Your own marriage, of course, put an end to that.' Thornton's voice held an air of humour.

'Still, I live in hope,' she returned boldly and met his stare.

And in that moment on top of the hill under the sun of a blue, blue Cornish day, something turned inside Caroline's chest. Something real and true and infinitely surprising.

She wanted it all to be true. His regard. His love. The sense of history that only real lovers ever had between them, keeping the world at bay, away, away, caught in each other's eyes and breathless.

Hating the sheer and utter impossibility of her life, she turned. She wanted to love him and she wanted him to love her back, for real, her earlier optimism dimming under the realisation that all this could only ever be a dream. For her.

Jennifer Ross was the sort of woman that he would marry. Connected, moneyed, and with an impeccable background, her parents melding the wealth of the Ross estate with that of Penleven.

Still, she had been asked to create an impression today and she was never one to back down from a promise, so when the others dismounted from their steeds to admire the view she stayed on hers, pleased when the Duke came over to her.

'Can I help you?'

'Indeed you can.'

Placing his hands about her waist, he lifted her down. She felt the full front of his body against hers and even when her feet touched the ground he did not let her go. The beat of his heart was slow and steady and she wondered what he might be making of her own accelerated pulse. Lord, he was a spy after all and damn clever and the heat in her face and neck must be a tell-tale sign of things being not quite as they ought.

Caroline frowned. The art of assuming the next character had always been easy in her life, but here the transition of status was unremittingly difficult.

'I am beginning to believe your ruse, Mrs Weatherby,' he whispered in her ear. 'Keep it up and we will have the Rosses gone in the morning.'

The lightness in his words was just what she needed. Laying one hand on his arm, she made herself stay still, giving the impression, she hoped, of a woman who was vying for more than Jennifer Ross was ever going to get.

'When are you planning to return to London, Mrs Weatherby?'

'I usually stay about a month, Lady Ross, and it was only last week we arrived back in this part of the country. Fortuitous, I thought, to coincide with your own visit, for otherwise I might not have met you at all.'

The weak smile she got in return was the result, Caroline suspected, of a woman who did not forget her manners even in the most trying of circumstances. Certainly, to a mother armed with the possibility of marrying off an eldest daughter to one of the richest Dukes in the land, her presence here must be more than galling.

'And your own family? Do you visit them?'

'Oh, no. My parents both died some years ago and it is just my brother and me left now.'

'And a child. We had word from a servant you have a child.'

Damn. Caroline had hoped to keep Alexander right out of this and she was therefore pleased when Thornton broke in on top of the conversation.

'There.' He pointed in the distance. 'If you look to your right, far in the distance is one of the fastest schooners you will ever see in the Channel. She's the *Sea Witch* and she plies the oceans between London and the Americas.'

Three pairs of eyes followed his finger and Caroline marvelled at the ability of a man who, even under duress, could conjure up a small and unnoticed thing as an excuse to change the subject completely. She supposed it came from his training, this careful observation of everything and anything around him, nothing unexpected or unforeseen. Even now he was turning the little party towards a low-lying peninsula and describing the beauty of the place that he named Lizard Point. And the mention of Alexander was completely forgotten.

* * *

They finally reached home a good two hours later and Caroline was exhausted from both the riding and the pretence. All she wanted was to sit on the chair in her room overlooking the sea, with Alex on her lap. She wondered how long it would be before Tosh came back as well, her slight uneasiness at any prolonged absence still very real after Exeter.

But the Duke of Penborne seemed to have other plans and as the Ross family retired to prepare for dinner he asked her to walk with him for just a few moments in the formal gardens at the back of the castle.

Tugging off his patch, he placed it in his pocket. She noticed that when they were alone now he very seldom wore it, preferring instead to squint his left eye if the light was harsh. His jacket, the collar of which was usually raised in company, was also dispensed with.

It pleased her, this lack of defence, and she smiled.

'Thank you for your help today, Caroline. I think Miss Ross may well be thinking any relationship with me a lost cause after your theatrics.'

'Your grandmother, of course, may be sorely disappointed. I think she would welcome the sound of more children in the castle.'

He laughed, but Caroline was not swayed from asking her next question.

'Why did Morag stay so far away from you when your parents died?'

He shrugged his shoulders in a peculiarly vulnerable movement and turned to the window. 'Because it was me who brought the illness of scarlet fever home to Penleven. From Eton. All of my family were dead and I survived. I think Morag knew that if she saw me then she would betray what it was that she felt.'

'Which was?'

'My father was her only child. She wished that it had been me lying dead on the chapel slab and not him.'

Shock and compassion overwhelmed her. 'How old were you?'

'Eight.'

Lord. No wonder he had left England at twenty and not returned for years. No wonder he was distant and solitary and dangerous. Life had taught him not to trust in anything or anyone. She weighed up carefully her reply.

'Alexander is not yet one. If he were to take ill and infect someone you loved and they then passed away, would you hate him?'

He looked surprised at her question. 'No. I would give my own life so that his should be saved.'

'And would have your father not have felt exactly the same?'

'Yes.'

'Well, there's your answer then.'

Running his hand through his hair, he turned towards her. 'I hadn't thought of it in quite that way before.'

'Because you were not a parent before.'

'Am I, Caroline? Am I Alexander's father?'

'You are.'

His fingers tightened around her own. 'My grandmother never stops telling me how like me he is.'

Another thought suddenly struck Caroline. 'Do you and your grandmother often share time at Penleven?'

He shook his head. 'No, we have not been close. In the past few years she has made Plymouth her home.'

'Did you ask her here because of me? Because of how it would look if there was no chaperon?'

'I did.'

Warmth and delight filled her.

'That's the nicest thing anyone has ever done for me in a long while and I thank you for it.' Taking his hand in hers, she raised it to her lips, tracing the edges of his knuckles with her tongue.

It was such a new experience to feel safe with someone else apart from Tosh that she savoured the feeling, Penleven bathed in the soft light of dusk and the flowers wildly prolific behind his shoulders. The noise of footsteps had him pulling away, his hands dropping to his side as he greeted one of the many gardeners, and their intimacy was lost.

He did not come to her that night either, though Caroline waited for him, the ring of a clock somewhere in the deep recesses of the house finally telling her that the hour was too late. Perhaps he had left the castle to go to

Holston or somewhere even further afield. Perhaps there was another woman, like the woman she'd seen him with at the Hilvertons', a less complicated woman, a woman who did not cry when he held her or think of impossible endings to a relationship steeped in inequality.

She could not think this, would not think this. Her fingers pulled through her mass of curls, bed messy and wild, the silken nightgown she had worn tonight clinging to her skin in a taunting way.

He did not come, will not come.

'No.' The single word was strangely comforting and she lay very still, listening to the tree branch against her window and the whispering of servants doing their final evening rounds.

Her former life seemed far away. She wondered if Penleven would have for ever ruined her with its luxury and easiness. Warmth. Food. Safety.

Penleven had a community of people whom she was beginning to care for and like, and her brother was looking happier than he had done in years.

She stretched, the silk sheets just another luxury. Tomorrow she would get her painting satchel out again and start to draw, a tableau of the castle and its inhabitants. And a memory of everything when she left.

Thornton heard the sound of laughing coming from the kitchen the next afternoon as he returned from a ride around the estate.

Usually the castle was a bustling place as servants got on with their cleaning and duties, but today Penleven was strangely empty, Henry missing from his station at the front door and James from the study where he usually waited to greet him after a ride.

He stopped and frowned as the sound of his housekeeper's voice boomed in delight. What on earth was happening? With determination he strode towards the kitchen and swung open the door.

James and Henry stood next to each other, sheaths of wheat artfully threaded through the lapels of their jackets and Caroline St Clair in front of them with her hair jammed beneath a lad's hat to stop the curls from falling into her eyes. A canvas set up before her was filled with rough outlines of almost everybody in that kitchen, the housekeeper in an apron, the small maid Polly holding a basket of lemons, two other serving girls behind her and the almost completed silhouettes of Henry and James prominently in the foreground. Marvelling at how she had with just a few lines caught the essence of everybody, Thornton saw Alexander in his cradle, the kitchen cat curled in the empty space on the floor beside him.

Penleven was being changed in front of his eyes, its quiet efficiency undermined by an onslaught of laughter and art and for the very first time since he had limped home from Europe he felt…out of place here. Too serious. Old, even.

Caroline looked up. 'Would you like to be in the picture, Your Grace?' she asked, a hint of amusement taking the sting out of the formal use of his name. 'This is just the drawing, but I plan to make it into a larger canvas and bequeath it to you all here at Penleven when I leave.'

'Leave? Indeed, Mrs Weatherby, without your presence here everybody might still be busy doing the jobs that I am paying them all for.' His impatience was belittling, but, with the fervour of a person who knew that they fought a losing battle, he kept going. 'My horse is outside, Henry, waiting to be brushed down. Get the stable lad on to it.'

'Of course, Your Grace.' Both twins hurried past him, but not before taking a quick look at the likenesses of themselves in Caroline's picture.

The other staff returned to their duties and even the cat woke up, removing itself from the warm softness beside Alexander's cot.

Caroline just looked at him, her charcoal still poised. 'I seem to have lost my models. Will you pose for me?' He had to smile at the sheer temerity of her question before shaking his head.

'I am still waiting for my portrait of Alexander.'

He mentioned nothing about the one that he wanted of her and saw the hurt in her face when she registered the fact.

Today he could not be kind. He had missed her these last nights, missed her warmth and her smiles and the particular way she had of holding on to him when she fell asleep after making love, her fingers entwined about his as if by their very grasp she might keep him there with her until the morning.

Tired of his poor humour, he turned away and walked out into the gardens, annoyed at seeing the Rosses already there, enjoying the sunshine. The Earl disengaged himself from the family party and came his way.

'If this is a good time, I would like to have a word with you.'

Thornton's heart sank because, in the face of the man opposite, he saw the beginnings of a conversation that he did not want at all. A discussion on the varying merits of his daughter.

Shepherding the Earl into the formal garden, he was relieved to see that his wife and children were only a little further off in the distance enjoying the fountain in one corner of the display. Perhaps he could make this relatively quick after all.

'Jennifer is coming up to a marriageable age and she seems to have a *tendre* for you, Your Grace.'

'Tendre?' Even the word was ridiculous.

'Feelings. She has feelings for you that she finds quite strong. As her father I thought it only right to approach you to see whether there would be any way in which you could reciprocate these feelings.'

Thornton was pleased by the question as it gave him

such an easy out. 'I am afraid my feelings are placed elsewhere, sir.'

'I see.'

Donald Ross looked crestfallen and disgruntled, a dangerous combination in a man with a daughter who was spoilt rotten.

'I suppose it is Mrs Weatherby who holds your affections?' His tone implied it would be easier giving Jennifer the bad news were he to be more specific than vague.

'Indeed it is, though I had not thought myself so transparent.'

'Not you, sir,' he replied quickly. 'Her. My wife has the knack of seeing a woman in love and she tells me Caroline Weatherby certainly shows all the signs.' He carried on as Thornton frowned. 'And a damn fine-looking woman she is, I have to say.'

Distracted, he nodded and greeted the Ross family as they joined him.

A woman in love?

Lord. Could that be possible?

Jennifer Ross looked at her father hopefully and when he shook his head she burst into noisy tears and ran in the opposite direction. Her mother trailed her with the nursemaids behind, the other children hanging on to their skirts. When Ross shrugged his shoulders, Thornton felt a strange sense of empathy for him. He was a father, after all, who was only trying to do his best.

Would he not be the same should he have a daughter? The very thought made him bid Ross goodbye and head for the house. He needed to apologise to Caroline for his boorish behaviour in the kitchen not half an hour earlier.

She was in her room painting, though when she saw him she quickly covered the canvas.

Alexander watched her from his place on the bed, the cat from the kitchen cuddled down by his feet.

'You do not wish me to see it?'

'It isn't finished. I never show unfinished works to anyone.' She barely looked at him.

'What of the picture in the kitchen.'

'That was only a drawing. A quick drawing.' With care she put her paintbrush down on a palette. Still looking away, the blonde in her hair caught the light of the sun, the indent of deep dimples in her cheek. *A damn fine-looking woman.* Ross's words came back to him as he sat down on the bed next to his son.

'The Ross family will be leaving in the morning. I have just had an interesting conversation with Donald Ross.'

'You have?'

'He seems to think that his wife has extraordinary powers.'

A frown marred her brow as she turned towards him, obviously interested.

'He says that she is able to distinguish a woman in love.'

'Her daughter?'

'You.'

Anger darkened her eyes and brightened her face. 'I have never heard of such a gift.'

'Is she right?'

'I am a mistress, Your Grace. One who will go to "a cottage in the village" when you tire of me. I have not the luxury of falling in love.'

'So she is wrong?'

She looked him straight in the eyes and answered, 'She is wrong.'

When he left, Caroline merely turned back to her canvas, removing the cover hiding the painted amber eyes of Thornton Lindsay.

'Damn you,' she whispered beneath her breath, smiling to reassure Alex as he looked up at the sound. 'And damn the stupid and interfering Margaret Ross for imagining herself a seer in the art of love.'

With care she added the last touches to the portrait, shadowing the background to illuminate the face and dabbing at the canvas in an attempt to create the illusion of depth. The earthy tones of the painting were exactly right for capturing Thornton Lindsay's dark golden eyes, and the muted light cast from the window behind him seemed to accentuate the roughness on his cheek.

One finger reached out and traced the lines that crossed the left side of his face. Today in the kitchen she had felt anger within him. And isolation. He did it to himself, this way he had of standing aside from people, of keeping up his guard, of being the lord of a place even in a sunny kitchen that had smelled of pies and oranges.

Thornton Lindsay. Thorn. Even his name was prickly.

And yet when he turned away she had also felt a certain hesitation, even longing.

Sighing, she massaged the tightness at her temples.

What had Margaret Ross seen? Crossing to the mirror, she searched her face.

Anguish lingered in the depths of her eyes. A woman who would never be a wife. A mistress who had been a virgin.

And one of the few people in the world who knew exactly what had happened to Lillyanna de Gennes.

Adele Halstead had been standing at her back and the girl before her, Tosh further away beside another group of unknown Frenchmen.

'If you go down that hill you will die, Lilly. You are French and your parents would be looking down from the hereafter with pain in their eyes in the knowing that Thornton Lindsay has consigned hundreds of good French folk to their deaths. Why do you not understand that?'

Hatred of anything British was easily heard in her voice and Caroline watched as the trajectory of her gun had lowered to the vivid scarlet red of the British soldier's back one hundred yards from them.

Thorn. Walking without a limp.

She had not known him then. Had not understood the anguish in Lillyanna's voice or her quick decision to run to him, placing her body in the line of fire. Protecting. Shielding.

Adele had sworn soundly and in the eyes of her mother's friend Caroline had seen something...wrong. Something dreadful. Some awful knowledge of what was going to happen before it did.

'Come back, damn you, Lilly. Come back.'

The girl did not turn once, her long blue skirt billowing in a freshening wind before she entered the church where the other English soldiers sheltered.

One minute and then two. Even the birds seemed to stop singing and listen as the rolling clouds hid the sun and the world exploded.

Horses. The sound of cannon fire. Screaming. They had run, she and Tosh, whilst the air uncoiled around them, run for the shelter of the forest where it was still possible to hide, stopping finally under an oak tree, the harsh and ragged wheeze of their breath the only sound filling the moss filled glade.

'She threw her life away,' Tosh had said finally.

'For him.' Caroline had returned and saw firsthand the power of a love that was prepared to sacrifice everything.

'Everything,' she said quietly to the woman reflected in the Penborne mirror five long years later. And knew, had she been in Lilly's shoes, that she would have done exactly the same to save him!

* * *

Thornton hit the bottle in the library and drank more than he had in a long, long time, the gathering hours of wayward thought settling on the one thing in his life that he knew was good.

Caroline.

She did not love him. She had said so to his face. Donald Ross had been wrong.

Upending the glass of brandy, he liked the feel of forgetfulness as it ran down his throat, melding the ghosts of the past into faceless nothings, the fierce strength of their presence softer in the amber glow of brandy. Diluted into calm.

Quiet.

Only shadows of what had been.

Carefully he pushed up out of his chair, hand against the wall to steady balance as he walked to the window.

Night, almost.

Another night.

And then another one.

And all he wanted was Caroline St Clair with him, around him, next to him, warm against his back and protecting against the nightmares that had him up after midnight pacing the floor.

The explosion as Lilly had kissed him, her body full against his own and waiting. No warning except the rapid beat of her heart and a certain knowledge he could remember in her grey-green eyes. Not quite honest. Hiding fear. Anger made him shake, the sweat on his forehead beading in a familiar tremor and, cocking his head, he breathed in and out, willing away panic.

Memories of another time hovered on the edge of his awareness, a long ago time when he was young and happy and Penborne had held the easy echo of joy. Before Eton. Before Europe. Before his skin had been shredded by the shrapnel of molten lead.

And Caroline. A light amongst the darkness, a flame in the ashes of what his life had become. Protecting him, from everyone.

He placed the bottle that he held on the table. Melancholy was a shady drinking companion and today he could barely stand himself sober, let alone stone-damn-bitter drunk.

Caroline had been painting. He tried to remember the glimpse of canvas that he had seen before she had covered it up. Another secret.

He was not even surprised.

'Lady of secrets,' he whispered and liked the sound of it, shades of Lancelot and the court of Arthur and the haunting beauty of Guinevere. Could she ever love him?

Damaged beyond repair. His face. His heart. His trust. His honour. And only Caroline could mend him.

She had to love him, because if she didn't he would be lost. Adrift. Irrecoverable.

* * *

She heard the door handle turn, slowly, carefully and the curse that followed the noise of the hinge.

Thornton.

He was here, in her room, leaning against the portal and finding his bearings, swaying drunk.

She could smell the brandy even from this distance, and see the tremor in his hands as he lifted them to the candle still burning bright on the mantelpiece.

His portrait lay covered and she knew the exact moment that he lifted the canvas, for his breath was drawn in.

'Why are you here?' Whispered.

'To...apologise.'

'For...?'

'Everything.'

She could only smile. 'Everything is a lot to apologise for.'

He came closer and sat down on the bed, bringing one finger to his lips as Alexander stirred.

'Shhhh...'

He placed the candle on the table, watching it for a moment as it wavered and then caught again, strong in the breathless silence of night. Not careless of fire and flame. An ingrained learning.

His eyes turned to her own, intense and measured, his teeth white against the darkness as he spoke.

'I wanted...the Ross woman's...words to be true.'

Slurred in a voice not quite his own. Given in confidence, quietly.

Hunger flared and caught. The unevenness of his skin in relief against the candle-glow, shadows of pain thrown into ridged cold grey.

'There are things that I have done…bad things…that you could not like and England needed done. But with you…I feel whole…good…and when she said it, the Ross woman…when she said the words, I wondered… hoped…' Question ripped uncertainty wide open on his face and in the depths of his eyes was just a little piece of the agony of war.

His war.

He had been positioned between armies and intelligence, balancing the local needs of one kingdom in danger of invasion against another whose Emperor ran rampant across all of Europe.

She sensed that he did not quite know what it was he was saying and so she chanced it. Chanced the words that he might not remember come the morning, but needed now.

'I love you.'

Simple.

Joy. His laughter broken as his mouth came down, nothing held back in the lips that slanted across her own. Seeking.

'Love me, sweetheart.'

'I do.'

She made no quiet response, no gentle ladylike carefulness. Opening her mouth, she revelled in the feeling of his tongue against her own, close, close and closer, his fingers threading through her hair, twisting her hard against him, breath erratic in the force of passion. Time stopped.

Still.

Suspended between a languid intense stab of wonder, her whole body vibrated against the connection of her soul against his.

Their first kiss!

Wildness released her from restraint. More. She wanted more, no longer careful but barbaric, frenzied, free. In the violence of their need for each other, the glass of water on the table knocked to the floor, breaking into a hundred shards, sharp and glistening, like her heart, never to be put back together, but scattered and dispersed by a feeling she had no sway over. And still he took her, hard, hard pressed as if he might never let her go.

Pain and ecstasy, close, entwined. The feel of his tongue against her own and the harsher nip of teeth. She bit him back and he swore. Fighting. Truth. The sharp pain of love unravelling everything.

'Lord,' he said when they finally drew apart and the world slid back into a recognisable shape.

'Lord,' he repeated as he slumped down on the bed, his eyes glazed in wonderment as the sleep that tore at equilibrium claimed him, slaked by confession, hope, relief. And brandy.

He awoke with a headache that would have made mockery of any hangover cure. And he awoke in his own bed, the blankets pulled about him and his shoes removed.

Even the curtains had been drawn.

James? Henry? No. The recollection of Caroline was distinct. And a painting. Of him? Honest. Open. Not quite him.

Moving his head, he groaned, placing his neck against the pillow and gradually regathering his balance.

He'd been in the library amongst the memories of Europe and the brandy that made it all distant.

Hadn't he?

A candle. Dancing against the gilt bright of blonde hair.

I love you.

She'd said it. He was sure.

Had he said it back to her?

Lies, deception and guile were the touchstones of his life so far. And suddenly he just wanted it all to stop.

I love you.

No trace of deceit in that.

None either in her dark blue eyes as he had tipped up her face to his.

'God, help me,' he prayed for the first time in a long time, the spirit of the celestial infinitely reassuring, reminding him that he was not alone.

When Henry came in with a glass of something he had concocted to help a headache, Thornton took it gladly.

'Where is Mrs Weatherby this morning?'

'She was just here with her son, asking after you.'

'My son,' he corrected and saw the flare of interest in the eyes of his butler.

'And the Rosses left just after dawn. There is a letter of thanks on your desk, Your Grace.' He crossed to the window to pull the curtains.

Thornton smiled. The Rosses gone, his headache going and the lingering sound of Caroline St Clair's voice on his mind.

I love you.

'Could you find Mrs Weatherby and ask her to come and see me.'

'Here, sir?'

'Here, Henry.'

She came ten minutes later. And alone.

'I hope your head is not too sore this morning.' There was a tone in her voice that was foreign, shy, and a wave of protectiveness engulfed him, throwing him off balance. On the right sleeve of her blue gown was a dab of rich red paint. Jarring memory.

'You made a picture of me.'

'It is not quite finished…'

'I liked it.'

She smiled then and the sunshine that had been hidden behind cloud all morning broke through, illuminating her hair blonde gold. Like an angel. His angel.

For the first time in her company he felt…nervous? Like a young boy in the attendance of a girl.

'I remembered other things too.'

She looked up, but did not speak, and he faltered. Unsure. 'I broke something.'

'A glass. It is of no importance.'

'And if I said anything at all that was offensive, then I am sorry.'

'You did not.'

'I was a paragon?'

'Of restraint.'

Both of them began to smile. A shared joy. Another first. Laughing with a woman in his bedroom on a bright morning, the promise of anything possible.

He saw how the fingers on her right hand kept fingering the gold bracelet on her left.

'Thomas gave you that, didn't he?'

She nodded. 'When I was twelve, and we had returned to Paris. I had been ill, you see, and he had been worried.'

'How ill?'

He was surprised when she paled.

'It was not Eloise's fault, you understand, or Thomas's.'

'How ill?'

'I got shot.'

'The scar near your left hip?'

'It was an accident. We were hungry.'

'Hungry?' Now he had lost her again.

'We lived in a cottage for six months on the north coast whilst Eloise journeyed west.'

'With her lover?'

She did not answer that question, but in her eyes Thorn could glean the truth. 'As children we had little idea of money and what she had left us was spent. Thomas shot a rabbit and I was cleaning the gun when it went off.'

'Who else was with you?'

She looked him straight in the eye and the fear he saw there nearly broke his heart.

'No one.'

Lord. The thought of it had him sitting up, the sunshine gone from his day. 'How long were you ill for?'

'A long time.'

Two children left on their own to survive. The bracelet a gift of the fact that they had.

Still were. Together. He thanked Thomas St Clair beneath his breath and resolved to have a talk with him that very evening. With care he reached out and took her hand, all form of teasing about last night gone.

'I will protect you,' he said and meant it. Not linked with lust or need or want. Her short nails made him smile. And he smiled again as her fingers curled in around his own.

'Where was Alex born?'

Suddenly he wanted to know everything about her. About them.

'At Hilverton. Thomas helped and the Campton midwife.'

'I wish I had been there.' His words surprised him.

'You were in spirit, Thorn. I kept on screaming your name.'

'Hating me?' There was amusement in his tone.

'Until Alexander was born. After that I could only ever thank you.'

Thank. Not love.

He was astonished as to the depth of his need to hear the words she had said last night.

I love you.

To his face when he was not drunk. For him to answer. Now.

'Who brought me back to my room?'

'Me.'

'Alone?'

'You took directions well.'

'And you tucked me in? I am sorry for the need—I don't usually drink as much.'

'You have given me protection, Thorn. Sometimes it is good for one's soul to reciprocate the offer.'

'Protection,' he murmured, leaning against the cushions at the back of his bed, a new resolution forming.

'I was engaged to be married once. Did you know

that?' He frowned at the way quiet anger was oddly juxtaposed against his need to tell her. All of it. His life that had been, and still was, secrets stored in the deep places of regret, secrets that had eaten at him for too many years.

When she did not answer he carried on. 'I thought I knew Lilly. I thought that I knew who she was until she followed me into a church in Orthez and blew us all up.'

Caroline blanched. Paper white. Her bottom lip shaking in fright.

'I am sorry if this distresses you.'

She shook her head and in her eyes there was suddenly something that made him stop. Cognisance. Knowledge. No mellow sorry this, but complicity. His mind began to reel with theories. Oh, Lord, that she should betray him, too. He felt sweat prickle beneath the light cotton of the sheets and a hollow ache of sorrow.

'She did it because she loved you.' Caroline said the words quietly.

'Pardon?'

'Tosh and I were there with Adele Halstead. She had a gun on your back and I think she would have shot you if Lillyanna had not walked towards you in the line of its fire. I don't think she had any idea about what would happen either, for from where we sat we could not see the horses with the cannons.'

'You were there?'

She held up her hands against his fury. 'It is not as

you think it was. Adele said that she would take us back with her to England when we came across her outside Orthez. Our mother had died, you see, and the offer was…enticing. An easy travel in a wealthy woman's carriage or a dangerous trek alone across the mountains into Spain. We were just in the wrong place at the wrong time, two seventeen-year-olds wrapped in the fabric of revenge and intelligence unknowingly, and when we did understand what was happening, we ran.'

'Lord. You are telling me…'

'I think that Lillyanna was set up. I don't think she knew anything at all about Adele Halstead's true plans, but she loved you enough to risk her life. And lose.'

Thornton brought one hand across his eyes, shading utter hurt and relief. He was glad for the fact that she kept on talking.

'If I were to have a guess, I would say that Lillyanna was expendable. Adele Halstead did shout out to her to stop, but she just kept on going towards you.'

The clock in the room marked the passing of silence. One moment and then two.

'Thank you for telling me this.'

Caroline nodded her head. Thorn's voice held an edge of tiredness and exhaustion. A bottled-up ache. An old wound. With the legacy of the brandy and the new knowledge of Lillyanna's sacrifice, he probably needed some time and space to assimilate the truth.

Not betrayal.

Only love.

'In the bureau behind you, in the third drawer down, there is a picture wrapped in green velvet. Could you possibly get it for me?'

Crossing the room, she did as he bid, resisting the urge to unwrap the material from the image as she handed it to him.

'Is this what you are after?'

He held it for a moment as if taking a breath, as if finding the courage for what he was about to do next.

'I just wanted to be certain…' he began '…certain that it was Lillyanna that you saw.'

The fabric fell away from the face of a woman he had once loved.

Caroline nodded. 'It was her.'

'I am glad that it is so.'

'You had the portrait commissioned.'

'No. Her brother left it for me after she was killed. Sometimes it has been a curse.'

'Because you cannot move on…?' She knew too well about the ties that the dead wrapped around one.

'Not that,' he returned quickly. 'Just that there were always questions, uncertainties about what had happened at the church. About betrayal.'

'And now they are answered?'

He smiled.

'And now they are answered.'

Chapter Fourteen

Thornton was standing by the window looking across at the evening sea when Thomas knocked on the door of his library.

'Your servant said you needed to see me, sir.'

'I think you and I need to talk.' Caroline's brother's eyes were guarded, his position on the edge of the sofa neither relaxed nor still as his fingers drummed, exposing nervousness. At that moment Thorn felt immeasurably older than the young man opposite as he took breath and paced before him.

'I would like to ask you for your sister's hand in marriage.'

The spluttering told him Thomas St Clair was clearly astonished by the words.

'You have asked Caro already?'

'No. Good manners insist that I talk to you first.' Thornton hesitated before continuing, mulling over the nickname that had been used. 'As her only relative I thought it was right that you should know of my intentions.'

'Caroline is in no position to marry you—the St Clair name was sullied by my mother when she ran away with—'

'What else?' He dismissed the argument with barely a thought.

'Our days in London would be remembered and you would be the subject of much gossip.'

'I have been that for all my years now, and it has never concerned me before. Besides, your disguises would protect you from memory. Even I could barely recognise Caroline without the red wig.'

'And as the Weatherby widow?'

'I am certain that we could live with that. Pious. Moral. Virtuous. Until she met me and threw it all away. What person in the world would not forgive her that were I to marry her?'

Silence greeted his statement and Thornton turned to the window and tried to catch his breath. He was suddenly aware that there was more and he did not want to know it, did not want knowledge and fact to distort what he felt now, ruining the memory of their kiss, or of her kindness.

It was Caroline whom he needed to hear this secret from. Not her brother. He wanted to see her eyes as she said it and understand her part in whatever had transpired.

'If your sister would like to talk with me, I will be

here for the next few hours. I also give you leave to discuss the topic that I have raised.'

'Very well.' Thomas held out his hand, grasping Thornton's own in a surprisingly strong grip. 'If I could have chosen a brother-in-law, it would have been you.' Sincerity shone from his face, but at the edge of that was guilt. *If I could have...* Past. Finished. When he got up to leave, Thorn did not try to stop him.

Caroline walked across the hills as fast and as far as she could, the wind splaying her hair and the tears spilling down her face.

He wanted to marry her.

He wanted to protect her.

And he had waited for her in the library as she had cowered in bed, not even trusting herself to get out of it lest she just kept walking into his arms.

And killed Thomas in the process.

So she had stayed away and locked her door. And late into the night when the candle had burned away to nothing he had knocked. Twice.

And then left.

Her heart thumped in her chest and her throat, the landscape blurred and empty. The cliffs she now marched along were endless, chalky soil, crumbling down into nothing but sea. Endless ocean and endless sky. Catching the hem of her skirt with the heel of her boot, she turned to a slight sound on the air.

A whistle of wind. She felt something close and strange before the world turned over. And her last thought before she fell was of Thornton Lindsay's proposal.

'Where the hell is your sister?' Thornton demanded of Thomas as he stormed into the room. 'She has been gone since this morning and Alexander is fretful.'

Thomas came to his feet. 'She didn't return for lunch?' Consternation laced his question.

'No one has seen her since she went out for a walk after breakfast and it is now almost three o'clock.'

'And last night? Did you speak about things last night, Your Grace?'

'No.' A single clipped word and silence

'She would never stay away from Alexander this long unless…'

'Unless?'

'Something was wrong.'

'Lord.' Thornton had the bell in his hand and was ringing it even as he strode from the room. More servants joined him as he stormed through the house, stopping only when he reached the front lobby. His cousin Leonard had also arrived unexpectedly that morning from London and had been the first to offer up his help, and his presence here was welcomed. Another body to help in the search for Caroline, and one who knew well the layout of the house and its lands.

'Mrs Weatherby is missing, Leonard. She has not

been seen since this morning around eleven o'clock and it is unlike her to be away so long.'

'Could she have gone into the village?'

Thornton looked back at Thomas, who shook his head. 'No. But I will send a servant to make certain.'

He took the middle of the floor and began to speak loudly to all who were gathered.

'Everyone else can leave their duties and follow me. I will assign you places to look. If she has fallen...?' He made himself stop. 'When you find her, send someone back here.'

Within ten minutes the room was emptied. Only his grandmother sat on the sofa, her ancient crepe-lined hands wringing back and forth against a wet handkerchief.

'She did not go into the village, Thorn. She was upset—' she began and took a breath to begin again. 'Upset when she left, for I caught her in the corridor. Just a short walk, she said, to clear her head, but her eyes were red and I could see she had been crying.'

'Did you see which way she went?'

'No, because I went into Alexander directly after speaking with her.'

'Then you saw what she was wearing?'

'Her red cloak with a dark blue velvet dress.'

Red. A colour easily seen from a distance or from the top of one of the high cliffs that bordered Penleven. Thornton made himself stop. She was missing, but she could be anywhere. Asleep in the library, perhaps, or in the gardens. As he strode through the front door, a steadily pouring rain changed his mind.

The barn, then, or the covered gazebo? Or the small cottage overlooking the sea. All these places would be searched. And he would find her!

'I could look in the fields behind here.' Leonard walked beside him, a building sweat on his brow and a glazed emptiness in his eyes. Lord, was he truly ill? Thornton could see his cousin wanted to tell him something, but he had no time for the problem as he ran to saddle his horse.

Cantering along the line of the cliff above Lizard Point, Thornton searched the deep fissures of land carved into rock. And saw nothing.

Dismounting, he tethered his horse before climbing down on to a ledge below the grass level.

'Caroline.' His voice was taken with the wind and returned to him as an echo. 'Caroline.' Loud. Futile. Hollow.

Climbing down further, he inched between the narrow ledges and called again. Still nothing. Thomas's voice sounded in the distance further down the coast. And away to his left up by the line of trees that led to the high fields more people ran.

Looking. Looking.

I love you.

'God, please help me find her.' His words, soft against the harsher panic.

He wanted to shout it like he was shouting her name, just in case…

In case what?

He shook his head and made himself think. He was a man who had tracked the enemy from Paris to Madrid and had seldom missed his target. He had been looking for Caroline foolishly, with his heart.

Now he needed to begin to use his head.

It was well after dark when he returned, the moon barely visible and the rain setting in.

Candles blazed at every window. Like a beacon he thought. Like a lighthouse. *Here I am. Come home.*

Thomas met him even before he had halted his steed.

'Any sign?'

'No.'

The look on her brother's face was the same as he knew would be on his own and he turned away so his heart did not beat quite so loud and so the tightness in his throat should again allow him breath.

'I will find her, Thomas. I promise you.'

Morag stood at the head of the stairs with his child and, shrugging off his wet jacket, he took the steps two at a time.

Alexander. In his arms. Close. Closer. The smell of baby and mother and hope all wrapped into one and the wet warmth of recent tears staining his shirtfront.

His child.

Their child.

Needing both mother and father. And afraid.

When he felt his grandmother's arm around his shoulders, he closed his eyes and prayed.

He didn't sleep. He lay with Alexander cuddled in against him and listened to the weather. Rain and wind and cold. And Caroline out there. Somewhere. Hurt.

It was three o'clock and only two hours before the dawn, two hours before he could begin his search again. The tiny fingers of his son closed around his own, and when he looked down, wide-open eyes watched him back, a tremulous smile wreathing his face.

'I will bring her home today.'

And he would. He promised himself even as he refused to give any credence at all to the niggling doubt of it.

Wet. Her face and arms and dress were all soaking wet. Caroline tried to stop the shaking and roll up on to her knees, but nothing seemed to be working and the darkness all around her was complete.

Drifting. Blurred. Pain. She let her head fall back and then she knew nothing.

Thornton's hands were bloodied as he scrambled up the cliff from the rocks. He had waded around from the beach and the barnacles had scratched him badly although the pain was hardly felt because he had caught a movement further up the cliff. Red cloth fluttering on the brambles.

She was here somewhere. He knew it. His heart pitched a huge jolt of relief when he saw only the ledges of rocks far below. No broken body. No trace of clothes or hair or blood.

'Caroline.' His voice wavered on the wind and he tried again. And again.

No response.

Climbing higher, he hauled himself up on to a narrow ledge, a few stray tussocks growing in the crack of rock and puddles of water in a fissure at the back. And then he saw her crumpled against the cliff not twenty yards from where he stood.

He could not even shout out as fear congealed words and robbed him of breath. Crawling across, he clung to the ledge, trying to find a foothold in the narrow space. Then he was there, beside her. As he lifted her into his arms she groaned, still alive at least. Tapping her cheek, he was relieved by her effort to sit up, the first movement he had seen her make.

'Easy,' he whispered, as a shower of small rubble was kicked up by her feet and flung through the air to crash fifty feet below on to jagged rocks. His hands searched Caroline's arms and legs and body for injury, finding the stickiness of blood pooling behind her left ear and running down her back. Lifting away her hair, pink from rain and blood, he cursed as he saw the scour line of a bullet where it had grazed her scalp. Another quarter of an inch…! He would not think of it.

The nearness of the escape winded him as he wrapped his arms tightly about her and held her, infusing his warmth into her coldness in an effort to stop the shaking.

'Caroline?' he tried again, swallowing as he willed her strength. 'Caroline. Can you hear me?'

She opened her eyes, the whites scrawled with redness. 'My head hurts.' Her fingers curled around his and she held on tight. 'And I fell. There was a sound…like a whip?'

'Can you sit up?' He did not want to scare her, so said nothing about the bullet. He needed to get her off the ledge and home and already the dark clouds forming above them threatened more rain.

'I think so.' She winced as he helped her and held both her hands to the side of her head. 'It hurts.'

'I know.'

'Where is Alexander?'

'With Morag at Penborne.'

'And Tosh?'

'Looking for you. Everyone is looking for you.'

'But I knew you would find me. I knew it would be you who would come…' Large tears welled and fell down her face, relief and shock mixed together and she saw the blood from her head on shaking fingers. 'If I don't survive…' She stopped and swallowed.

'You are not dying, Caroline.'

'I'm not?' She wiped her damp tears with her jacket sleeve and sniffed. Loudly. And explored her scalp further.

'It's only a scratch.'

His anger heartened her. 'You call this a scratch?' Now that she was sitting up, she had her skirts raised as she searched for other injuries, turning her legs this way and that to make certain that everything moved. When she was reassured that nothing seemed wrong, her hand returned to her face.

'What of this?' Her first finger ran over a sizeable lump on her forehead. 'Do my eyes look normal?' Widening her eyes and turning towards the light at an angle, she looked to him for reassurance.

Without meaning to Thornton began to laugh, the tension of the last twenty-four hours suddenly taking its toll.

'Damn it, Caroline. You never ever do what I expect you to.'

She was still.

'I saw a man once in Paris with a bump just like this fall right over and just stop breathing and another time—'

'Enough.' He pulled her hand away just as the clouds burst and a deluge poured down across them. Removing his jacket, Thornton slung it across her shoulders, helping her to thread her arms through the sleeves and buttoning up the front when she had done so.

'We need to get down from here,' he shouted across

the noise of rain, pointing upwards to where a large section of soil seemed to be peeling off from the bank, threatening to fall across them and knock them off their tenuous perch.

She nodded, her already pale face whitening further as she stood. Thornton kept a firm hold on her arm as she took a few deep breaths and tried to calm her panic.

Bringing her behind his back, he instructed her to place her arms around his neck.

'Don't let go whatever happens.'

'I won't.'

'Good.'

He took one step out into space and heard a strangled scream of fear.

Caroline clutched Thornton tighter. If they died, at least it would be together, here, on the rocks beside the sea at Penleven. She felt his heartbeat loud against her fingers, no quiet even pulse either, but a hammering hard quickness, belying his calm exterior and his easy reassurance.

She could barely believe that he would be able to find a track down from this impossible position. But he seemed to, inch by inch. Foot by foot. The muscles on his arms bulged against resistance and the corded veins in his neck were a raised black blue.

'Nearly there,' he said softly as he rested for a second, laying his forehead against rock and taking deep breaths.

'I could try to walk by myself—'

'No.' The word was barked sharp and she did not argue. Besides, looking at the descent he was taking, she knew she had no hope of managing it herself.

A bunch of brambles here. A rock that became a handhold there. Sheer guts and brute strength and a belief in himself that she found beguiling. When a trunk of old tree crumbled beneath his grip, she heard him curse and waited for the fall, but he clutched on to a thorny shrub nearby, the blood from prickles running down his hands and across the rolled-up sleeves of his shirt.

And then they were down, the last steps to the pancake rocks below, easy in their execution.

Tears welled in her eyes as she clung to him, true shock now setting in given their relative safety.

He had saved her.

He had risked his own life to save hers.

She smelled the sea and freedom. And love.

In his actions.

In his body.

It was in the strength and largeness of him, in the valour and bravery and fearless challenge of what he had done. No words yet, but something more.

Love.

Translucent in the pale light of morning, hanging on

the edge of death and shimmering wordless in the very act of sacrifice.

When his lips came down across her own, she leaned in and the world around them simply disappeared.

Chapter Fifteen

Caroline woke up the next morning and stretched. Everything ached. Her neck, her head, her legs—even the tips of her fingers where she had dug them into the soil to make certain in the night that she would not slip off the ledge into nothingness.

Thornton had not stayed with her, for the drink that the housekeeper had plied her with on her return had contained some sort of sleeping potion and this morning she felt a strange sense of disquiet. He had seemed angry with her. For slipping across the embankment, perhaps, and putting them in danger? She wished he would come and see her, for the clock on the mantel gave the time as well past eleven.

It was almost twelve when the door opened and he appeared, carrying flowers from the gardens at Penleven.

'My grandmother thought you would like these,' he said as he laid down the vase on her bedside table. 'She picked them with Alex this morning and sends her love.'

'And Thomas. Where is he?' Suddenly she felt the same dread that she had after his disappearance in Exeter.

There was a second of silence.

'He left for Plymouth this morning.'

'What?' Sitting up, she pushed the bed covers from her legs, her whole world skewered into fear. 'Why? Why has he gone there?'

'He said something of a man he needed to see. I did offer him a coach and driver, but he was adamant in his refusal. He took a horse from the stables and left after dawn.'

Panic claimed her. Lord. She suddenly knew why he had gone. Thomas thought that the de Lerins had something to do with her fall, that was why.

A fall? Her fingers went to the space behind her ear. 'I didn't just fall, did I?'

'No. You were shot at.'

'And Tosh knows this?

'He does.'

Everything fell into place. His anger. His disappearance. Her brother was going to France to find the de Lerins and give himself up so that something like this would never happen again. He was going to make certain that she was protected. She knew it to the marrow of her bones.

Her heart raced. Could she ask Thornton Lindsay for assistance? He was a man with contacts and skill and the father of her child. Would the connection between them be enough to make him break the law entirely and help?

And then what?

Face the de Lerins virtually alone? She knew how honourable he was. If Tosh was to be incarcerated for the killing of a man with no principles, she was certain Thorn might well take the whole affair in his own hands and do away with those left who still threatened them.

Horror consumed her. *Don't give him the chance to do so,* a small voice churned inside. *He has already given more than anyone should be asked for his country and for his King. Make him stay. Make him safe. For Alexander's sake and for mine.*

Utter calm claimed her and she sat down, lying back and placing her hand upon her forehead.

'I feel ill…' she just managed, trying to make her voice shake and her tone plaintive.

'I'll fetch the doctor?'

'No. It's just that I can't help remembering…everything…the fall…' Closing her eyes to shut out probing amber eyes, she groaned. 'Perhaps if I slept I'll feel stronger…' The warmth of his fingers scored the back of her hand. A last touch? A final goodbye that he did not know he was making? She resisted the urge to turn her palm over and hold on as a lump formed in the back of her throat.

'I shall return in an hour or so and see how you fare. Is there anything at all that I could get you?'

'Just…need…to sleep.'

As soon as Thornton withdrew from the room she stood, pleased that the woman who had been sitting with her did not return. Alone. At least for the time it would take to escape from Penleven and follow her brother.

Thorn found the letter pinned to Alexander's cot less than three hours later.

> Please can you look after Alex, Thorn. He likes to be cuddled in the morning and sung to at night, and when he goes to sleep he needs his red woollen blanket next to him.
>
> Don't follow me.
>
> With love. Caroline.

His howl of anger brought his grandmother into the room and, when she had finished reading the note, her voice was steady.

'You will need to fetch them both back, Thornton, for we cannot do without them. I made a mistake in not coming to you all those years ago because my heart was broken. Don't you make the same one with Caroline.'

'You will stay here, then?'

'For as long as you need me. I am sure that Leonard would be glad to stay as company.'

He liked the feel of her hand on his arm. Family. It always came back simply to that.

Grandmother to grandson. Father to son.

And Caroline. If he lost her, he knew that nothing would ever be right again.

Plymouth was bustling with people and he scoured the streets and taverns for the only two that he wanted.

They had to be here somewhere—the first ship to France was not departing till the morning tide and there had been no sailing at all across the Channel since the very early hours.

Where would they have gone? He kept his eyes peeled for a white filly and her sable sister, both steeds missing from Penleven. Eight o'clock now. He had been here since six and the churning worry of not being able to find them in time was growing. Had Thomas lied about his point of departure? Were they in some other port town, finding a way across the Channel? His mind skipped across the possibilities. Lord, it could be any of a number of villages along this part of the coast.

Raucous cheers from a nearby watering hole drew him inside. Thomas was keeping a roomful of people entertained by reciting the more lewd poems of Robbie Burns as he played cards. His sister, dressed as a youth, stood behind him, guarding his back.

Hardly ill. Barely recognisable. His blood boiled with the evidence of her brazen lies and the fear, that had been his companion from Penleven to Plymouth, crystallised into something else entirely.

Rage. Savage and powerful.

Duped one time too many by a consummate deceiver.

He wasn't even cautious in the way he sat at the table, ignoring the St Clairs altogether as he asked for the hand to be dealt.

Twenty minutes later, when he had amassed a sizeable part of the winnings, Caroline settled at the side of her brother. Unexpectedly she too asked to be dealt in, her face as bland as hell. He couldn't remember ever playing another person who gave so little away and when she won the first play he was not surprised. Just another secret that she had kept from him. Just another skill that a conwoman might need as she wreaked havoc in the lives of lesser men before moving on. Caring for no one.

She did not sew or knit or darn.

She did not sing or play an instrument.

She was not interested in the planning of a menu or the setting out of a favoured garden.

Not these woman's pursuits, the soft gentle accomplishments of a well brought-up lady.

No. Caroline played cards as well as any sharp he had ever met and was able to take on the persona of another with an astounding ease. Here, with her hair tied back in a queue she was…more than believable. It was in the way she swiped her sleeve against her nose as she sniffed and took an easy swallow of brandy in the glass before her, before calling this hand.

A challenge.

He met it.

Laying down three kings and an ace.

Her three aces and the joker trumped his easily and when the onlookers dispersed as she gathered her winnings he stood, tired by the pretence of it all.

'I have a room in the coaching inn around the corner. If you are not there within half an hour, I will have you both arrested as horse thieves. Do you understand?'

'Yes.'

When he walked out, he hoped that they knew the game was up.

They arrived at the inn within fifteen minutes. Caroline had reverted to the costume of a woman again, her cloak draped across her shoulders and inviting more than a little attention.

She looked beautiful. Scared. Lost.

All around the entrance hall men stared at her.

'Alexander?'

'Is fine. Morag has taken it on herself to look after him until I am back.' He refrained from including her in the equation.

Shepherding them up the steps and into his room, he

was glad for the fire that had been lit in the hearth and the bread and wine laid out on the table.

'Have you eaten?'

'Not for a while.'

Thomas's voice was wary. Resigned.

'Then help yourself.'

Neither twin did so.

'How is your head, Caroline?' He had seen the twinge of pain on her face when she had inadvertently brushed the cloak against her neck as she had slipped it off in the mounting warmth of this room.

'It is fine, thank you.' Polite. Formal. Infinitely distant.

'I presume you have acquired a passage to France?'

'We have, Your Grace.' Thomas's turn now. 'On the *White Swan*. She leaves on the morning tide.'

'Why?'

Silence.

'Is it because you are chasing the person who shot at Caroline?'

Silence again.

'And is that person the same one who took you hostage in Exeter?'

He was close. He could feel it and see it in the thin pulse at Thomas's throat. Markedly faster.

Caroline was better at hiding everything! She stood, looking straight at him, a hint of anger in the tip-tilt of her chin. Wishing him away.

Nothing made sense. But then it never had with the

Anstrettons. Or Weatherbys. Or St Clairs, he corrected himself. Accomplished liars with myriad identities.

'It seems to me that we are at an impasse, then.' Crossing his legs, he leant back, pouring himself a generous drink as he waited. He had had enough practice with the emotions of guilt and deceit to know that it took very little to induce an outpouring once you had uncovered the true root of its cause.

With a flourish he extracted his timepiece, a quarter to nine. If he had anything on his side, it was time.

Caroline felt dizzy and she laid her hand against the side of the sofa to keep her balance. Today dressed in his riding clothes and sitting in this beautiful room, Thornton Lindsay looked...at home. Just as he had in the gaming room in Plymouth, his ease at playing cards amidst the company of people he usually avoided startling.

He was a chameleon, adapting to what life threw at him with an astonishing ease, the scars on his face the only sign of a time when things had gone astray. And he was clever. Already she could see his mind assessing their destination and their reason for flight.

He was a King's man, a soldier, versed in the arts of war. Right and wrong would hang in shades of black and white with such a man and a life like hers with no strict codes of conduct or discipline would be wholly foreign to him.

Her mother had flitted from person to person and

from place to place, a gypsy and loose, any restrictive morality sacrificed to her own personal needs and tailored to want.

Any want!

Guy was one such case in point. Beautiful and deadly, like some giant exotic reptile crawling through their lives, he had invited comment and interest. How their mother had loved being the centre of attention after so many years of being on the outer circle of everything.

For once she was envied! She would not leave him because a hundred other women wanted him, no matter what he did! That was the way of people with no moral fibre. They became trapped by their ineptness and greed and buried by their inability to ever quite do anything right.

They had been fourteen when their mother had met him, in the autumn of 1809. Eloise had gone to a ball with one lover and come back with another, her red dress exposing ample charms. They had seen her from their hiding place beneath the stairs when she had returned, seen her laughter and her thrall, seen the danger on his face and the way he did not quite meet her eyes, seen the marks on her neck where he had pressed too hard.

Lord!

Her life.

Their life.

No wonder it had come to this!

Angry shame consumed her.

'There is nothing at all you can help us with, Your Grace. It would be far better if you were to return to Penleven and forget us altogether.'

His eyebrows rose up as he considered her statement.

'And our son. Should he also forget you altogether?'

'No.' Her voice shook. 'When we can come back, we will—'

Thomas stood suddenly and interrupted her. 'I think it is time for the truth, Caro, for if Alexander should suffer…'

She knew the look in her brother's eyes. Familial duty. It had been there before in all their moments of need.

'I murdered a man, Your Grace. I am returning to France to confess it.' Flat. Categorical. 'I planned on leaving Caroline behind, but she has insisted on coming too.'

Caroline felt her world spin and stop. Pulling her brother's arm hard, she turned him around. 'He does not know what he is saying. It was not him.' She shouted the words. Loud. Too loud. She saw confusion on Thornton's face and resignation on Tosh's as he continued.

'I hit him hard on the back of the head with a marble statue until he fell. Until he did not breathe.'

Stop. Stop. Stop. Desperately she laughed, hearing an unbecoming edge of hysteria on the edge of it. 'He does not know what he is saying. It is the wine, perhaps, or—'

'Why?'

One simple question. She could barely look at the Duke. But it had to be answered because otherwise her brother would be completely lost and damned, held solely accountable for an act that had saved her.

'He almost raped me.' There. It was out. Said. Raw in the sunlight of this room. Unreal amidst the polished furniture and fine velvets. 'At Malmaison one Sunday afternoon when prayers had finished…'

The events of that day were engraved in her memory, never to be forgotten. She hated the way her breathing quickened and the damp heat of shame beaded beneath her clothing.

'How old were you when this happened?'

'Seventeen.'

'Hell.' He stood and walked towards the window. 'Hell,' he repeated.

'He had tried before.' Pulling back the sleeve of Thomas's shirt, she pointed to a wide band of wrinkled skin. 'He had hurt us before. Many times!' Her breath came in strange gulps and she swallowed to contain absolute panic.

'You think this was your fault?' Thornton Lindsay seemed even more dangerous than usual. 'You were forced into an act of self-defence against some loathsome lowlife and have been on the run ever since. And you think to explain your actions to me? To apologise?'

Caroline blinked. Was he implying…? Did he mean…? She could not quite understand his message.

'Why the hell would you even think of going back?'

Tears blurred her vision.

'Guy de Lerin's family have kidnapped Thomas and shot at me. If Alexander were to get in the way by mistake…'

She didn't finish.

'What was the name you mentioned?' Interest flared in Thornton's eyes.

'Pardon.'

'The name of the man you think you killed. What was his name?'

'Guy de Lerin.'

'Guy de Lerin? A man with dark brown hair, a moustache and a mark on his lip, just here.'

Both Caroline and Thomas nodded.

'He is dead, but *you* didn't kill him. Guy de Lerin worked for General Soult in France, and his throat was slit after accosting the daughter of a Spanish landowner a few days before I met up with Adele Halstead in Orthez. I know it was him because I received his sabretache and its contents from a local who was more than unhappy with the pretensions of Napoleon and his troops.'

'My God.' Tosh sat down heavily on the sofa, trying to ingest such a revelation. 'My God. I didn't kill him?' Tears welled in his eyes and Caroline sat down next to her brother, taking his hand in her own.

'You are sure that it was him?'

'I never forget a name or a face and good intelligence was only ever about memory.'

An altered truth. Dead, but not by their hands.

'This changes everything.' Caroline framed her statement in the way of one who could not quite take in the changing of circumstance.

'It certainly does, though there is one small problem.'

Both looked over at Thornton as he spoke.

'Somebody out there is still trying to kill you.'

They travelled back to Penleven with hired horses pulling the coach to give the horses they had ridden to Plymouth a rest.

In the aftermath of their revelation there was a strange silence between them.

Trust. Distrust. Honesty. Dishonesty. Their confession had left them feeling uncertain and Thornton Lindsay wasn't making any of it easier as he sat opposite them and looked out of the window.

Catching Thomas's glance, Caroline saw the same puzzlement on his face that she was certain must be on her own.

Laying her head back against the cushioned seat, she momentarily closed her eyes, exhausted, with hope and worry, and from the sheer and utter weight of her love for the man opposite.

If Tosh hadn't been sitting next to her, she would have risked rejection and moved across to sit next to him, but with her brother here and the very real chance of a rebuff, she stayed where she was.

The Duke's hands were still scratched from his

search for her on the cliffs, and the mark on his forehead where a rock had hit him was red raw and raised. And today in the inn in Plymouth when he had guided her through the lobby with his arm against the small of her back, she had felt that familiar bolt of warmth. Safe. Protected. Cherished.

'Do you still have the locket that you retrieved from the Halstead house?'

She frowned even as Thomas nodded.

'I wonder if I might look at it?'

'You think it holds a clue?'

'It's something from your past and the attacks did not begin until after you had taken the trinket.'

'You think it is Adele Halstead?'

He did not answer.

Caroline tried to fit all that she knew of her mother's friend into some sort of a pattern, her head still reeling from the fact that they were now free to be whoever they wanted to be.

No longer murderers.

No longer running from the law.

Caroline and Thomas St Clair.

The tight knot of uncertainty dissipated. Whatever happened from now on could be faced because Thomas's life was no longer suspended in the fear of recognition and accusation.

'Was there anyone in Campton that you were at odds with?'

She shook her head at the same time as Thomas did.

'What about in London? Did you tread on anyone's toes unduly?'

'Excelsior Beaufort-Hughes, perhaps? He felt he should have been allowed Caroline's hand in marriage. And I played a number of card games and won. Some of those I faced may not have been happy with the losing, though I never cheated. Could it be someone there?'

'At the moment I am as much in the dark as you about motive.'

'But you think they will try again?'

'At Penleven you will both be safe.' He barely looked at them as he said it and Caroline felt the full force of the weight of his duty settle around them.

Just that. Just duty.

With a half-smile she nodded her gratitude and turned away, hating the tears that sprang to her eyes and the aching regret in her heart.

Chapter Sixteen

Caroline pulled the wrapper more firmly around her shoulders as she climbed the stairs to Thornton Lindsay's room. It was late. Almost two o'clock, and the noise of the servants had stopped some time ago, the house wreathed now in silence. She clutched the locket in her palm, glad she could use it as an excuse to come to his room if all else failed.

Slipping inside the door, she took a breath and was surprised by the sound of his voice.

'Who's there?'

He was not asleep. The light of a small lamp bathed an adjoining room; when she walked a few steps more she saw him sitting at a desk, a pen in one hand and a glass in another. A fire burned dully in the grate and on the wall in front of him was a picture of a beautiful woman. The artist in her was instantly interested in the lines, colour and strength of the work.

'My mother had it done,' he commented as he saw her looking. 'As a gift to my father just before she died.' He buttoned up his shirt where it gaped open across his chest as he saw her looking. 'Why are you here?'

'I have the locket of my mother's that you asked for.' She placed the trinket in a small silver dish on one end of his sideboard. 'And I wanted to say thank you for coming to find us and for bringing us here to Penleven with you.'

'This is the third time I have brought you home, Caroline. Will you be staying or is there another charade that is yet to play out?'

Removing himself from her proximity, he walked to the table, lifting a large brandy glass and emptying the contents. He looked wary.

'I thought I knew you. But every moment I know you less. And I am not certain that I can survive more lies.'

'You think that of me?'

'This morning you were a woman who lay back against her pillow and feigned illness before stealing a horse from my stable and chasing her brother over half the county. Today dressed as a lad you were a card sharp, and tonight, in nothing save a smattering of lace and silk, a siren comes to my room when the house is quiet.' He shook his head and faced her directly. 'Who am I to believe is you? This person, that person? I spent years on the continent watching my back and trying to determine the truth amongst myriad lies. And all I want now is honesty. Can you give that to me, Caroline, for if we are to have any chance at giving Alexander a family, there needs to at least be trust between us.'

Trust.

Not love!

'If you would prefer that I leave…'

'No. I would not prefer that.'

The clock on the mantel ticked loud, marking the seconds of silence between them. Awkward. Heavy. She wished she had not worn this nightdress, its inherent thin silliness so suggestive of what she sought, and of what he refused. Embarrassment swamped her, the red bloom of blood a tell-tale sign of shame.

'There is one more thing that I think you should know.'

He turned towards her. Warily.

'My mother always said that our father was from the English aristocracy, though she would never mention any name.'

'Why not?'

'She had washed her hands of England, I think, and did not want us going back to be laughed at, or criticised. Besides,' she added beneath her breath, 'Mama was not a woman who limited herself to be the exclusive property of just one man.' The bleakness of the truth fell between them again. A mother who was a trollop and a father who could have been anyone.

Unexpectedly Thornton began to smile.

'Could you promise me, Caroline, that there will be no more secrets between us?'

'I could.' Her voice shook.

'I asked your brother for your hand in marriage. Did he tell you that?'

She nodded, hating the hope that was beginning to bloom inside her.

'And yet you locked your door and didn't answer it.'

'I thought if you knew about de Lerin, you might follow us and kill him yourself. I was trying to protect you.'

'So you are saying…?'

She took a breath and risked it. Risked everything.

'I love you, Thornton. I've always loved you since the first moment of meeting you at the ball in London with your collar up and your one eye daring the world to comment.'

'Comprehensive!'

She frowned. It was not the answer that she was wanting back. Not at all.

'I love you, but I can only marry you if you love me back.'

He began to laugh.

'Do you truly not know how I feel, Caroline?'

She shook her head and in response he brought her hand to his mouth, his tongue laving a singular thin pain of passion that grew from her groin and blossomed. Quicksilver heat!

'I have loved you since that first night when you came in your white gown and healed me. I had not been with a woman for more than two years...'

'And I had not been with any man before.'

Lord! Suddenly he knew exactly what it was she was saying. The succession of lovers and husbands was as much of a cover as everything else in her life and she had been a virgin when he had paid her fifty guineas and forced her into his bed! Another secret! And with this one, guilt racked the very fibre of his being.

It had only ever been her and Thomas against a world that had labelled them as outcasts because of their very lack of alternative. And he had used her as his mistress.

'You were a virgin?'

'Yes.'

Everything made sense. Her fear. Her tightness. The blood he had seen on her ripped petticoat as he had stuffed it into the fire.

He could barely breathe with the fineness of such an unexpected gift.

'I love you, sweetheart. Nay, don't cry! 'Tis my heart I am offering you and that's the truth of it.'

'I don't know if I deserve it. There are things that I have done...'

'As the Duchess of Penborne, no one could touch you, I swear it.'

'And Thomas?'

'Will have a tongue of land nearby on the coast and build a house of his own.'

Tears streamed down her face.

'You would do that for me? For us?' Tracing the line of scarring up his cheek, she leaned in, kissing the hurt away, her tongue careful in its passage, a quiet touching. 'I like it how you do not wear your patch with me or pull your collar up high. When I first met you, I thought your eyes were like those of a falcon.'

'Blinded?'

She laughed. 'No, amber and dangerous.'

'And predatory?' He began to peel back her thin wrapper, his brows rising when he determined how little she had on underneath.

Caroline stood completely still, waiting as the clothes pooled at her feet. In the candlelight with his eyes upon her she felt beautiful. Loved. Cherished. Sensuous.

She laughed as he lifted her up into his arms and brought her to his bed. In a moment he had joined her, his clothes also discarded on the floor.

Heat engulfed her and the throb of want drummed heavily, like it had right from that very first time in London. And when his hand came between her legs to open them, she arched into his touch and welcomed him in.

It was dark when she next awoke, the candles blown out and the light beat of rain steady against the window. When she moved she knew that Thornton was not next to her. Confused, she sat up and saw him, leaning against the wall by the fireplace and smoking a cheroot, its small red ember easily seen in the night.

'You cannot sleep?'

He flicked the smoke into the fire and stretched. 'Did your mother ever tell you anything else about your father?'

Of all the questions he could have asked, this was the last one that she expected, and she tensed further when she saw the locket and a small knife in his hand.

'Once at Malmaison, she told me that she believed God provided a soulmate for everyone and that she had squandered her chance.'

'And you were born in…'

'1796.'

'In France?'

'Yes.'

He pushed away from the wall and came towards her, a smile replacing the frown that had been there.

'Eloise St Clair arrived in France in the winter of 1795 according to the information I have gathered from the shipping lists. Do you know if your mother had known Adele Halstead for long before she died?'

'No. She came to Paris when Mama was ill. They spent a lot of time together talking, and I think she helped my mother come to terms…with everything. That was one of the reasons we did not denounce her when we found the locket and other jewellery missing.'

'And when you came to London you tried to get these things back?'

'Only the locket. Mama was always careful to take it with her, you see. It was the only possession that she truly treasured.'

The tone of his voice made her hesitate. 'You think Adele Halstead could have something to do with…' She did not finish because in the fog of uncertainty another thought suddenly congealed. 'You think that she knows something about who our father is?'

'More than something. I think she came to Paris knowing exactly who your father was.'

'Because…?' She could no longer follow any of his reasoning.

'Because it is my guess that your father is her husband, Maxwell Halstead, the Earl of Wroxham.'

He placed the small portraits of herself and her brother before her. Caroline saw that they had been carefully removed from the locket, their edges still curled from many years of placement.

Silence settled between them and she waited as he lifted the lamp and opened the trinket to the light so that she could more properly look inside.

Her mother's much younger face stared out of the roundness, and the other held the portrait of a boy.

'The man is Wroxham. Do you know the woman?'

'It is my mother. They were beneath our likenesses all of this time?'

He nodded and history fell into place.

Her fingers entwined around his. 'When did you know?'

'Nothing is ever truly coincidental, Caroline. And Adele Halstead is not a woman to be trusted. Did your mother know she was married to Wroxham?'

'I am not certain. I never heard her speak of her life in England and she did not use the name Wroxham or Halstead in Paris. She called herself Madame de Chabaneix. It was only by chance that we saw her here in London as Lady Wroxham in the gardens at Kew, though we were careful not to let her see us.'

'From my information Wroxham married her in Spain in 1801. He had bought a commission as an officer there and she was already "helping" England with intelligence about the French.'

'Do you think he knows? About her?'

'I am sure that he does not, though the better question would be what was the relationship between your mother and the Earl.'

'Eloise always said that she had loved him.'

'How old was your mother when she had you?'

For a moment Caroline counted back the years. 'Nineteen, I think.'

'Under age for a marriage then in the church, though there was always Gretna Green.'

'You think they could have eloped?'

He shrugged his shoulders and stood up straight. 'If

he had married your mother, Adele Halstead would have strong motive to be rid of you.'

The truth crystallised with a stinging clarity. 'Because Thomas would be the heir to the earldom? My God. He needs to be told about this.'

'If he is, it will probably be dangerous. The bullet missed your brain by less than a quarter of an inch. I think it is safe to say that whoever shot at you wanted you dead, and Thomas is inclined to rush into things.'

'Whoever? You don't think it was her? Adele Halstead knows how to handle a gun.'

'Yet she has been nowhere near Penleven in the past month. I have had her followed since the locket incident and there has been nothing in her movements to arouse suspicion.'

'And Tosh? Why wasn't he killed in Exeter?'

'I am not sure.' His eyes flared in interest as she brought his hand up to cup the full softness of her breast. 'But I will find out.'

'Tomorrow. Think on it tomorrow, Thorn, for I need you now.'

Her simple invitation was quickly taken up as he gathered her body to his own in the bed.

'You are telling me that you think we are the offspring of the Earl of Wroxham?' Lifting the locket to the light, Thomas peered inside. 'So what happens now?'

'As I see it, we have two choices. You could stay here at Penleven—'

'Where we have already been attacked once.' Her brother's impatience was easily heard. He had been incredulous when Thornton had told him of his theory about their father and the meeting here in the library this morning had tilted him from disbelief to anger.

'Now that we have identified the risk, it will be easier to protect you.'

'To stay inside, you mean. To be guarded and hidden—'

'My grandson only means to keep ye both safe.' Morag Lindsay got up from her place near the fire, the pain on her face reflecting old bones that no longer moved as they once had.

'Safety at what cost? For how long would we be prisoners?'

'I think you are overreacting, Tosh…' Caroline tried to distil her brother's anger and Thornton overrode them both.

'Your brother makes a fair point, and this brings me to plan number two. If we played Adele Halstead at her own game, we might indeed have more luck. Morag will introduce you into London society as the children of one of her great friends and she will make certain that the Earl and his wife are included in the dinner party.'

'I don't understand.'

'Wear the locket around your neck and see if the Earl

has any sort of reaction. Often attack is a better policy than being defensive.'

Morag began to laugh, slapping her hands against her leg and cackling gleefully. 'Ahh, Thornton. You are getting more and more like your father.'

'Thank you.'

Caroline wondered if he should have taken such a statement as a compliment, but with the possibility of Thomas finding his place in the world she did not wish to express even the slightest notion of doubt.

Besides, she knew that they were playing this game according to the rules of a master. Thornton looked neither worried nor perturbed by the situation, and his confidence in coming out with a result by following this course was beginning to find favour with her.

'We can open the family house in Mayfair,' Morag was saying. 'Leonard could come too, and of course we must visit a modiste and have some clothes made up for you both. And a hairdresser and a dance master.'

Lord. Caroline caught Tosh's eyes as the old lady continued to rattle off a long list of helpers, and when he smiled back the most extraordinary thought hit her.

We were born to this! This extravagance and excess. After so many years of penny pinching and being careful the notion was bittersweet.

Chapter Seventeen

Caroline was dressed in the most ornate gown she had ever seen. It was of blue silk because, according to Morag Lindsay, 'she was too old to wear white'. The buttons down the back were fashioned from pearls, and at her neck she wore her mother's locket.

She made herself stay still as she waited for the woman sent out from the London modiste to finish pinning the last alterations. After the woman had done so, Caroline was flustered to hear Thornton's voice downstairs. They had spent every night together since coming to London, but he seldom came to his grandmother's town house in the daytime in an observance of society rules and she wondered why he should be here now.

A maid brought in a note and gave it to her and she read it quickly. He wished to meet her as soon as she was able in the salon downstairs. With care she tried to hurry the highly strung French seamstress, but it was a good half an hour before she was finally able to join Thornton.

He was alone, standing against the window looking out, his patch across his left eye and his collar drawn up. And in that singular moment Caroline understood what it must have cost him to be here, amidst the tittle-tattle of society and the gossip that he hated.

'I am sorry to be such a long time.'

He took her hand in his and drew her against him, close, the slight pressure of his fingers a silent communication between them.

Together. Just them.

'I wish we could go home.'

'So do I.' The tone in his voice worried her and she looked up.

'Is there a problem?'

'I am not certain,' he answered and drew away, shutting the door that was open behind them. 'I went to see the Halsteads yesterday and whilst Adele is undoubtedly devious, age and position have definitely mellowed her.'

'Perhaps she is resigned to the fact that she cannot change things, that the truth will come out.'

'Or perhaps it was not she who shot at you on the cliffs at Penleven.'

Caroline felt her eyes widen. 'Who else could it have been? Who else is there?'

Anger sparked in his eye at her question, but there was also a puzzled dawning, a realisation that was crystallising even as she watched him.

'My grandmother has Alex in the garden, Caroline. Could you ask her to your room on the pretence of some information you are seeking and stay there until I come for you.'

When she nodded he looked relieved, the prickling sense of danger slightly diminished.

'Give me an hour and I promise that I will tell you everything. And keep to your room with the door locked until you hear my voice.'

And with that he was gone.

Morag grumbled all the way from the garden to Caroline's room, the stick she used to help her get around punctuating the conversation as they climbed the stairs. The town house had never seemed as big as it did today and Caroline was pleased when the last steps were reached, for Thornton's whole attitude had made her wary, his deductions about Adele's innocence leaving them wide open to danger.

'I am not quite…as agile as I once was…if you could just give me a moment.'

Her rasping breathing pierced the silence and, holding her son very closely, Caroline wished with all her might that the old lady would hurry. She resisted the impulse to take up her hand and drag her along because she did not want to frighten her and had no real idea as to how she could explain the rush.

Thornton's cousin's shadow fell across them just as they came to the beginning of the last corridor.

'Why, Leonard,' Morag said, as she turned to rest against the solid wall behind her, 'you gave me quite a fright—we were not expecting you back until the evening.'

In the dull light Caroline could see a glistening sweat on Thorn's cousin's upper lip, and his eyes were unusually dilated, a smell not unlike sugar permeating the air. A familiar scent!

Was he ill? Had he been hurt somehow? A darker thought crossed the others when he did not answer, but continued to observe them.

Opium. Guy de Lerin had been a proponent of the drug and she knew now where she had smelt that particular sweet pungent aroma before. She moved in front of Morag and pushed Alex into her arms. Lord, and look what opium had made him do!

'I need to speak with Leonard for just a moment, Your Grace. Could you take Alex to my room and wait for me there?'

The old lady looked surprised at the request, but relief blossomed in Caroline as the woman did as she had been asked and shuffled off. Ten minutes since Caroline had seen Thornton. How long would it take him to realise his cousin was back, for she was suddenly certain that Leonard Lindsay was dangerous? Plastering a smile across her face, she gaily began to talk.

'I am so glad to have this opportunity of finding you alone, Leonard, for I wish to have a surprise party for your grandmother's birthday in another month and I was hoping that you could attend. I had thought something along the lines of a small soirée here, though, of course, if you think she might prefer a celebration at Penborne, I could keep that in mind.' She hoped such ramblings had given Morag the time she needed to reach her room, but did not dare to turn around and check.

He looked puzzled.

'I know you are a busy man and there are a lot of other social occasions on in London, but perhaps...' She made a point of looking past him, clapping her hands suddenly over her mouth. 'A spider, there behind you. A huge spider.'

When he looked around, she ran by, pushing him off balance. But he did not follow her and in that second Caroline knew that she had made a fatal mistake.

Alexander. It was Alex whom he wanted.

Horror consumed fear.

'Thorn,' she shouted and began to retrace her steps, screaming a warning to Morag as she came through the door to see what all the commotion was about.

Thorn's grandmother fell like a puppet pulled on

some unseen string, back and down, crumpled still, Alexander's cries from behind her.

And then everything went black.

Caroline came to in a carriage, a sturdy rope around her wrists. Two men she did not know sat opposite her, and in the arms of the one with a ring in his ear Alexander lay sleeping. Her heart, already racing fast, began to race faster and fear consumed her, tightness constricting her breath, and her cheekbone was throbbing.

'Why are you doing this?' She barely recognised her voice.

Neither answered.

'I will give you double what you are being paid. Triple if you just take us home.'

Lord. Her eyes flicked to the other man, hoping to see some humanity in his face, some humanity that she could appeal to. But his visage looked as uncompromising as his cohort's.

'If we took you home, lovie, no doubt we'd be seeing the bars of a prison for a long time to come.'

'Then let me down at the next town and I promise that you will be amply rewarded. I give you my word that it will be so.'

Both laughed. 'The payment for depositing you in a brothel in Gloucester is payment enough and no strings attached.'

She blanched.

'And my son?'

'An orphanage will take him.'

He leaned over and ran his thumb across the downy skin on Alexander's cheek and horror crawled down Caroline's spine.

These men were mad. She was in a carriage with her son heading towards God knows where with two men who were mad.

'If it were me, I would think about taking my chances on a generous payment from the Duke of Penborne. He would reward you amply were you to bring us home and I promise you no questions would be asked about your involvement in any of this.'

'The man who gave us the gold said this is what you would say. He said you were only the Duke's mistress and that he would never marry you. He said that you held no sway at all over the purse strings of the Lindsay fortune and that Thornton Lindsay was tiring of you already.'

'And you believed him?' She scoffed at the words and then watched in horror as the man without the earring took something from his pocket. A bottle with the words 'Tincture of Opium' written upon it. When the world lost shape, her last sight was of Alex crying as he heard her pleading groans.

She woke in a room painted dark indigo. As she tried to focus, she realised that the dress she had been wearing was gone, replaced instead by a petticoat, the décolletage falling drunkenly across the line of her nipples.

Swallowing, she held her head very still as jagged lines of ache plundered through her temple, though the locket around her neck swung into view as she moved and her hands came up to release the catch.

They had not taken this? She could barely believe her luck. Alex lay on the bed beside her, asleep. She felt for the pulse at his throat in a sudden dread and was relieved to find a steady and normal rhythm. Just asleep then. Now, if only she could find something to write with. The fire held scraps of newspaper and she stood, carefully walking over to the grate. Already she could hear voices outside and hurried to her task. A piece of charcoal and the edge of paper. And a name.

Property of Thornton Lindsay, Duke of Penborne.

Folding the scrap, she opened the locket and placed it inside. And then she lifted up her son and deposited the trinket in the folds of cloth that swaddled him. *Please, please, God, let someone find it. Because if they didn't, all would be lost.*

The door opened and a middle-aged woman stood there, hair a bright and flaming red and the clothes she wore were the ones that Caroline had come to this place in.

'My name is Clara,' she said quietly, 'and you are in Gloucester. You should bring in a good amount of business with skin like yours, even given the fact that you are no longer a virgin.'

'Business?'

'It's a brothel, my dear. Even a well brought-up girl such as yourself should have an inkling what goes on inside such a place. In four days' time the master of the place will return from London and he will be pleased to have you first.'

'You cannot mean to do this—' Caroline began, but the woman stopped her. 'I would never willingly—'

Her arms were suddenly behind her back, stick-hard fingers opening her mouth and the same bitter tea that she had been forced to drink in the carriage was poured cold down her throat.

'Willingly, nay. But drugged with laudanum, my dear, it's a different story, and after a few months, what man would want you back…?'

'Thorn.' The word was torn from fear and dread and aching love.

And the last sight she saw before her eyes closed was the crone lifting up her son and leaving the room.

She was tired and could not quite use her arms or her legs, but a man was there undressing, one hand making free with her, his cold fingers opening her thighs, pushing in.

Not Thornton. Nothing was right.

'Pleeease…' She tried to beg.

'I'm almost there, my sweetling. How refreshing to encounter such eagerness in a new girl.' When he smiled she saw half his teeth were missing and the rest were yellowed dirty.

His other hand lifted the sheets, the gleam in his eyes easily seen in the candlelight as her breasts fell away from the flimsy lace. As he lay down beside her, the hardness of his sex brushed against her leg. Waiting, but not for long. She saw that in the lust on his face and in the shaking eagerness of his loathsome hands.

And then the door swung open, wide, the sound of anger and hard knuckles against a soft face, shouting and blood on the sheets. Red, red blood.

Hers?

She tried to focus, tried to rise, but she could move nothing. Neither her eyes nor her mouth nor her hands.

Death. Was this it? This heavy lack of breath, and darkness, and a gurgling rattle.

'Caroline?' Her name came from far away through a passage of light. And then she could breathe again as a weight was rolled off her.

'Caroline.' Again. Closer. Worried. She shook her head and the world cleared a little.

Thornton was there, taking in her battered face with a darkening fury. And behind came Tosh and a taller blond man. Somehow familiar?

'Caro?'

Tears gathered and ran in warm silent runnels down her cheeks. Thornton. Beside her. Real.

'He nearly…' she began, looking up as she reached out, and when his arms closed about her strong and true, the horrors of this place broke upon her in a wave.

'Alexander…?' The word was a shrill desperate sob.

'Is at Penleven Castle being well looked after by Morag. Your note was found, sweetheart. He is safe.'

'It…was…your cousin.'

'I know. He shot himself when I confronted him a few moments after you did, but by then you were gone.'

'And Adele?'

'Knew nothing about any of it. Her crime was only that of greed.' Pulling a blanket around her shoulders, Thornton waited as her shaking lessened and Thomas began to explain.

'Mama had asked Adele Halstead as a Frenchwoman living in London to contact the Earl of Wroxham. She gave Lady Wroxham the locket as a way of reminding him of who we were.'

The tall blond man suddenly laid his hand on her brother's shoulder and began to speak.

'I am Maxwell Halstead, Caroline, and I am your father. Perhaps you will allow me to explain it.'

'Father?' Suddenly Caroline could see the lines of the boy from the locket in the face of the man.

Without being asked to, he reached out, taking her hand in his own. Warm. Big. Solid. A father. No longer orphans and perhaps even loved? The tears in his eyes told her it was so. Her eyes. Deep blue. Dependable.

'Your mother and I were married briefly. We eloped, you see, to Gretna Green but it was only a matter of hours before my parents caught up with us.' The shaking in his voice told of the effort it was taking him to relate the tale. 'I was eighteen, just eighteen, and my mother had a hold on me then that I am now ashamed of.' He stopped, giving the impression of one who was carefully finding words that would be kind. 'Eloise St Clair was a girl who loved anything of value and the money my mother offered her to just disappear was substantial. When she ran away to Europe, the Wroxham gold made certain that there would be nothing said here to tarnish the reputation of the earldom.'

'Yet she had us.'

'I swear I did not know that she was pregnant until Thornton brought Thomas with him yesterday to Wroxham House and I knew without doubt that he was my son. If I had known that, I should have followed her to the very ends of the earth to retrieve you.'

'Your second wife...made no mention...of the locket?'

Thornton broke in. 'Adele Halstead left England this morning, Caroline. She was the one who kidnapped Thomas in Exeter, but who at the last moment could not find it in her to kill him. For that alone we gave her leniency to leave the country and begin a new life elsewhere without the law on her tail.'

Adele Halstead gone and Leonard Lindsay dead. An ending to it all. And a new beginning.

The three men who meant the most to her in all the world stood as one solid wall of muscle and safety and the tension dissipated as she smiled.

'When did you know…about your cousin?' She addressed this question to Thornton and he knelt down beside her.

'After visiting Adele Halstead, I tried to work out who had been around you each time there was an accident. Yesterday morning the answer came to me. It was Leonard, but when I went to confront him in his room he wasn't there. The maid told me he was in the garden and by the time I returned—' He stopped and she heard the shake in his voice. Husky. Desperate.

'I love you, Caroline. If I had lost you…' Her fingers curled about his and she held on.

Like she would for ever.

Generations spanning the years. Her father and mother married!

A circle.

A whole new family and growing bigger all the time. From two had come three and now she was certain that another child was forming.

A girl.

And her name would be Lilly. A sister for Alexander.

Without even meaning to, she began to cry.

Epilogue

'How did you find me, Thorn?'

They lay in bed in an inn in Gloucester later that night. Together and safe.

Beneath the sheets she wound her bare legs around his warmth and smiled as his arm came firmly round her.

'When Alex was deposited in a church by the dockyards, a priest found your note in the locket and a constable was called. Luck had it that the miscreant who had delivered him to the church was in his cups in a local bar and easily apprehended, and so the whole story came out.'

Caroline shuddered at the memory of everything. How easily it could have turned out differently.

'My cousin will never hurt us again, darling. It was a madness, I think, from the opium he had become addicted to. That, and a jealous envy, made him a lunatic.'

'Just suddenly?'

'No. On reflection it had been coming for a while, and he found it hard to let Penleven go. It had been his home, you see, for the years that I was away and he wanted it for himself. When he saw how much you meant to me and that Alex could become the heir, it tipped him over the edge.'

'Were you his only family?'

She felt him nod rather than saw it. 'Morag and I. His parents died when he was very young and he had about as much time at Eton as I did.'

'So you knew him there.'

'No. He was four years older than I am and our paths seldom crossed.'

She rolled on top of him, a thread of teasing in the movement, and his wicked smile made him look so breathtakingly handsome that Caroline had to smile back. In the candlelight his scars were only shadows and without his patch she could almost imagine him to be healed.

She hoped that he was, by her love.

Leaning down, she kissed his nose, his cheek, his temple.

'If anything ever happened to you, my darling…' His voice was rough.

'It won't.'

'Promise me?'

In response she lifted her locket from the table beside the bed and hung it around his neck. 'Tomorrow I will paint a portrait of us both inside.'

'To keep for ever,' he whispered back, opening his mouth as her lips came down warmly across his own.

Turn the page for a sneak preview
of the first book in the new miniseries
DIAMONDS DOWN UNDER
from Silhouette Desire®,
VOWS & A VENGEFUL GROOM
by Bronwyn Jameson

Available January 2008

Kimberley Blackstone didn't notice the waiting horde of media until it was too late. Flashbulbs exploded around her like a New Year's light show. She skidded to a halt, so abruptly her trailing suitcase all but overtook her.

This had to be a case of mistaken identity. Surely. Kimberley hadn't been on the paparazzi hit list for close to a decade, not since she'd estranged herself from her billionaire father and his headline-hungry diamond business.

But no, it was *her* name they called. *Her* face was the focus of a swarm of lenses that circled her like avid hornets. Her heart started to pound with fear-fueled adrenaline.

What did they want?

What was going on?

With a rising sense of bewilderment she scanned the crowd for a clue, and her gaze fastened on a tall, leonine figure forcing his way to the front. A tall, familiar figure. Her head came up in stunned recognition, and their gazes collided across the sea of heads before the cameras erupted with another barrage of flashes, this time right in her exposed face.

Blinded by the flashbulbs—and by the shock of that momentary eye-meet—Kimberley didn't realize his intent until he'd forged his way to her side, possibly by the sheer strength of his personality. She felt his arm wrap around her shoulder, pulling her into the protective shelter of his body, allowing her no time to object. No chance to lift her hands to ward him off.

In the space of a hastily drawn breath, she found herself plastered knee-to-nose against six feet two inches of hard-bodied male.

Ric Perrini.

Her lover for ten torrid weeks, her husband for ten tumultuous days.

Her ex for ten tranquil years.

After all this time, he should not have felt so familiar but, oh dear, he did. She knew the scent of that body and its lean, muscular strength. She knew its heat and its slick power and every response it could draw from hers.

She also recognized the ease with which he'd taken control of the moment and the decisiveness of his deep voice when it rumbled close to her ear. "I have a car waiting outside. Is this your only luggage?"

Kimberley nodded. "I assume you will tell me," she said tightly, "what this welcome party is all about."

"Not while the welcome party is within earshot. No."

Barking a request for the cameramen to stand aside, Perrini took her hand and pulled her into step with his ground-eating stride. Kimberley let him, because he was right, damn his arrogant, Italian-suited hide. Despite the speed with which he whisked her across the airport terminal, she could almost feel the hot breath of the pursuing media on her back.

This was neither the time nor the place for explanations. Inside his car, however, she would get answers.

Now that the initial shock had been blown away—by the haste of their retreat, by the heat of her gathering indignation, by the rush of adrenaline fired by Perrini's presence and the looming verbal battle—her brain was starting to tick over. This had to be her father's doing. And if it was a Howard Blackstone publicity ploy, then it had to be about Blackstone Diamonds, the company that ruled his life.

The knowledge made her chest tighten with a familiar ache of disillusionment.

She'd known her father would be flying in from Sydney for today's opening of the newest in his chain of exclusive, high-end jewelry boutiques. The opulent shopfront sat adjacent to the rival business where Kimberley worked. No coincidence, she thought bitterly, just as it was no coincidence that Ric Perrini was here in Auckland ushering her to his car.

Perrini was Howard Blackstone's right-hand man,

second in command at Blackstone Diamonds, a legacy of his short-lived marriage to the boss's daughter. No doubt her father had sent him to fetch her; the question was *why?*

* * * * *

Get swept away down under with the glitz and glamour of the Blackstone empire as Kimberley tries to determine the real reason behind her "reunion" with Ric....

Look for VOWS & A VENGEFUL GROOM
by Bronwyn Jameson,
in stores January 2008.

Stay up-to-date on all your
romance reading news!

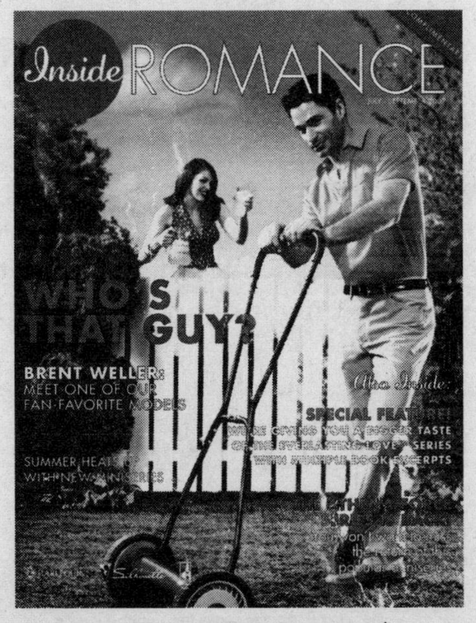

Inside Romance is a FREE quarterly newsletter highlighting our upcoming series releases and promotions.

Visit

www.eHarlequin.com/InsideRomance

to sign up to receive our complimentary newsletter today!

IRN1107

COMING NEXT MONTH FROM

HARLEQUIN® HISTORICAL

- **THE VANISHING VISCOUNTESS**
  by **Diane Gaston**
  (Regency)
  When the Marquess of Tannerton rescues a beautiful stranger from a shipwreck, he has no idea that she is the notorious fugitive the Vanishing Viscountess! Can he prove her innocence—or will his fight to save her bring an English lord to the gallows?
  RITA® Award winner Diane Gaston visits the gritty underworld of Regency life in this thrill-packed story!

- **MAVERICK WILD**
  by **Stacey Kayne**
  (Western)
  The last thing war-hardened cowboy Chance Morgan needs is a reminder of the guilt and broken promises of his past. But when pretty Cora Mae arrives at his ranch, her sweetness soon begins to break down his defenses.
  Warmly emotional, brilliantly evoking the Wild West, Stacey Kayne is an author to watch!

- **ON THE WINGS OF LOVE**
  by **Elizabeth Lane**
  (Twentieth Century)
  Wealthy and spoiled, Alexandra Bromley wants an adventure. And when a handsome pilot crash-lands on her parents' lawn, she gets a lot more than she bargained for!
  Join Elizabeth Lane as she explores America at the dawn of a new century!

- **HER WARRIOR KING**
  by **Michelle Willingham**
  (Medieval)
  Behaving like a demure Norman lady does nothing except get Isabel married to a barbarian Irish king who steals her away on their wedding day. She refuses to be a proper wife to him—but Patrick MacEgan makes her blood race, and she's beginning to wonder how long she can hold out!
  Don't miss this sexy Irish warrior—the third MacEgan brother to fight for the heart of his lady.

HHCNM1207